OCEANARIUM

P.K. HAWKINS

SEVERED PRESS
HOBART TASMANIA

OCEANARIUM

Copyright © 2023 Severed Press

WWW.SEVEREDPRESS.COM

ISBN: 978-1-922861-56-6

CHAPTER ONE

This wasn't the first time reporter June Reilly had been asked to meet up with a potential contact in a questionable time and place. Granted, that wasn't a common occurrence, either, no matter how much movies and books liked to act like hot news tips from anonymous sources always came in that way. Maybe it had been like that more once upon a time, but when June got an anonymous tip, which in itself wasn't really that common, it tended to be in the form of an email or text. Sometimes those rare tips led to her having to meet someone shady in a dive bar. Sometimes she was asked to meet in a parking lot, usually for the tipper to not even show up. That was especially true of the story she had been trying to pursue for the last year. People who had information about Dom Logane tended to rethink sharing it at the last moment.

But for all the peculiar requests and strange people she might meet in her pursuit of the truth about Mr. Logane, this was the first time someone had asked her to come alone at night to an area that made June honestly think she was about to get mugged, or much worse. The anonymous source this time had asked to meet her at the docks and shipping yards on the east side of the city, and to do it at two a.m. That kind of request should have been an automatic no from her, but she was getting desperate. She was being pressured by her editor, and possibly from people higher up in her news organization that wanted to remain nameless, to finally drop the Logane story once and for all. There was nothing there, they would tell her. Except she knew there had to be. If there wasn't, there wouldn't be any reason for everyone to want her to stop, right?

Her contact had told her to come alone, which was worrying and yet still sort of expected, but he had also told her not to park anywhere near their rendezvous spot. That could mean he didn't want anyone to see a vehicle around that could be traced back to her, but it could also mean he didn't want her to have an easy escape route. The location was the north side of a mostly unused warehouse right at the edge of the water, with large doors leading right into the harbor that made it seem like various small boats might be able to dock inside it. At first glance it might seem abandoned, but now that she was up close to it she couldn't help but think that the unused feel to it was deliberate, like someone had actually painted it to appear rusty or run-down from a distance. Her contact had told her the exact spot where to wait and not to deviate from that, and as she waited here she started to realize why: there were cameras all around this place, new ones that definitely seemed too high-tech for just another abandoned warehouse. There was definitely something going on here. She just hoped it was what she was actually looking for, and not some kind of trap to get her after all of her snooping.

And what exactly are you going to do if it is a trap? June thought to herself. Although she had been asking herself that question repeatedly for the last hour that it had taken for her to get to this point, she still didn't have an answer. She rarely did. June wasn't the sort to ever plan anything out in her life, an attribute that had been getting her in trouble from the moment she had first been able to walk. She just went forward and did whatever seemed right at the time. Maybe that was why so many opportunities and job promotions had eluded her. When you didn't think things through, the consequences never occurred to you until it was too late.

It was almost enough to make her want to change, to be a more careful person. Almost. She kept telling herself that at some point just going with her gut before she considered all the options just had to pay off. Maybe this would finally be the time.

But probably not.

Still, she knew there was a story here, a big one. Dom Logane was one of the richest men in the world. He came from inherited wealth, although he always talked in every interview he had ever given that he was self-made in a way that implied that he may not have ever met an actual self-made person in his life. He had gotten into software and communications when he was in his twenties, and that had increased his wealth to the point that most people probably couldn't comprehend the actual amount of money he had. And he had bragged about it in the media as often as possible.

Or at least he had until about three years ago. That was when he had stopped showing up in public, and anyone who asked where he had gone had a tendency to be silenced very quickly and definitively.

June's initial thoughts on doing an investigative piece on the vanishing of Dom Logane had been little more than flights of fancy. She hadn't really thought she was going to do anything on the subject. But when her initial simple and half-assed inquiries had been harshly rejected, she had slowly become more and more obsessed with the story. The surest way to get her to want to know more about a subject, after all, was to tell her she wasn't allowed to know.

After many, many months of increasing tension in her search for more information and a disturbing number of leads that had vanished on her right before she could investigate them further, she was finally here, waiting on a man she barely knew anything about coming to her with vague assertions that he knew something big, something crazy, something she couldn't possibly believe about the missing billionaire. And with nothing else to go on, she couldn't make herself ignore the lead even if it was fishy as all hell.

Waiting in the dark outside the warehouse, June tensed as she heard a door open somewhere around the side of the building. For the brief few seconds that the door was open, she could hear something inside like machinery, possibly some very large engine or motor. When the door shut, though, all sound ceased. Immediately June's mind began to race with possiblities. From where she was currently standing, she should have still been able to hear the sounds of activity from inside the building. That could only mean that the building had some heavy soundproofing, which shouldn't have been something anyone would care to install if it was as dilapidated as it wanted to look from the outside. There was definitely something suspicious going on within, but she couldn't make herself come up with any plausible idea as to what that activity might be.

She heard quiet footsteps coming from the direction of the door. June crouched lower just in case it was someone she really didn't want seeing her here, but as the sounds got closer to the corner of the building she heard the same voice she'd heard earlier in the day on the anonymous phone call that had tipped her off. "Ms. Reilly? Are you there? I've arranged to have the cameras along our route turned off for the next five minutes, so we have to hurry."

A part of June's mind warned her that this might be her last chance to turn around and walk away from all this. Whatever she was about to find out was likely something big and serious, and there was no telling how complicated her life was about to get or if she was going to be in any danger. But she only listened to that part of her mind long enough to register what it said and then say insulting things about its mother (which she supposed was actually her own mother, but whatever). That just wasn't the kind of person she was or ever would be.

"Show yourself," June called out, trying to make her voice be both loud and a whisper at the same time and instead turning it into a scared-sounding croak. "And don't try anything funny. I'm armed."

That at least was true. She had a small pistol in her purse with six rounds loaded into it. Just because she was one to make reckless decisions didn't mean she had to be dumb about it. She was going to make sure she had something backing her up just in case it came down to that.

After about a second of hesitation, a figure came around the corner of the building. It took a moment for June to see any details of him in the dark. He was an older gentleman, maybe in his fifties, short with a neatly trimmed beard and coveralls with small dark patches of dirt or dust on them. He didn't look especially intimidating. Just the opposite, in fact; there was something distinct in his posture that gave off the vibe that he was really nervous or frightened.

June kept her hand on her purse as she moved closer to him, ready to reach in and grab her weapon if the man made even the slightest threatening move. "I'm assuming you have to be the person I talked to earlier."

Despite his claim that all cameras were off, the man looked around as if he expected someone or something to be watching them. "We don't have time for me to explain too much. The door is going to seal in just under five minutes, and we need to be on the other side of it before that happens."

"What door?" June asked. "You don't really expect me to just follow you immediately with no explanation at all, do you?"

"If you don't, you're not going to get any of the answers I have for you. I'm not kidding around here. I'm putting myself in a very bad position for this, and I'm not going to mess around with it any more if you aren't going to at least trust me a little."

She wanted to say that this situation required her to offer far more than just a little trust, but he was visibly shaking as he spoke. This man really was scared, maybe even for his life.

"Okay, fine, I can trust you for the moment, but could you at least give me a name I can call you? It doesn't even have to be your real one."

"It's Maury. Now please, there's maybe three minutes left if you really want to know what Logane has been doing."

Those were the magic words that finally got her following him.

Maury led her back to the door he had come out of, his eyes darting every which way the entire time. He even looked up a couple of times as though he expected some camera or security drone to come swooping down on them. The door had a keypad next to it that Maury swiftly ran his finger over with a well-practiced code. He opened the door and went through, not bothering to hold it open for June and forcing her to rush to get in before it swung shut behind her. Once inside, the sound of machinery made it hard to hear anything else he said, and there were no lights on leading their way.

"Grab on to my shoulder," he said, or at least something like that. June couldn't be completely sure. "Follow me closely, and watch your footing. You don't want to trip and fall into the water."

Water? she wondered, but Maury didn't give her any time to question him on it. Instead, she did exactly as he asked. The sound under their feet changed from the solid thud of concrete to the light thump of wood as they walked over some kind of bridge. Then it was replaced with the clanging of some kind of metal.

"There's another door here, then a ladder," Maury said. "Hurry, the door is going to lock shut in less than a minute."

What the absolute hell am I getting myself into? June wondered. But she said nothing and didn't hesitate, instead going through the door. Inside there was just enough light to see that she was on a small platform with a ladder going down, with Maury already halfway down it. The door thumped behind her, and a few seconds later there was a mechanical click as it locked automatically.

"Okay, we're in," June said. "Could you please now explain…"

"Not yet," Maury said. "We're about to begin our descent, and we need to get out of the way of anyone who might see us."

Descent?

Oh crap, June thought. *I'm in deep now. Literally.*

CHAPTER TWO

"Are you telling me this is a submarine?" June asked. "Are we seriously on a submarine right now?"

They were at the bottom of the ladder in some kind of entrance hall, but June was too busy trying to make sense of what was happening for her to look around at any details.

"Yes, of course," Maury said. "It's the only way to get to the underwater theme park."

"Underwater theme park?" she asked. "Wait. No. That can't be right." There actually had been some rumors about such a thing in some of the conspiracy theory groups posting about Logane on the internet, but she hadn't entertained that idea in the slightest during all of her investigating.

"I'm pretty sure I mentioned it during our call," Maury said.

"I didn't actually believe you," she said. "I thought you were just some kind of nut job. I was just humoring you just in case you were, I don't know, trying to get the drop on me and slip a knife in my ribs."

This seemed to perplex Maury. "If you thought I was capable of that, why would you listen to me or follow me at all?"

That was a good question, one June wasn't sure she would be able to give a good answer to. She was acutely aware that the situation had been one that would have sent most women running for a well-lit street far away from the dockyards and Maury's cryptic talk. But desperation could make people do things they would never do otherwise. And working for over a year on the Logane story had definitely made her desperate.

"I guess I've just gotten to a point where I'm not thinking that far ahead anymore with this story. Thinking too long about following leads on it has led to a lot of those leads vanishing under mysterious circumstances."

"Yeah, well I probably should have vanished on you as well. Remember what I told you. We have to be calm and collected if we don't want to get caught. And we *really* don't want to get caught. Do you understand?"

She nodded that she did, but she was beginning to realize that she really didn't. Whatever was actually happening here, it wasn't the sort of normal illegal activity she had envisioned.

"Okay. Fine. But no more hiding info and being vague about what's happening. Now that you've got me on a fucking submarine going who knows where, I think you can at least give me some real answers."

"I will," Maury said. "Let's get some place a little more hidden first where we can sit down. It's going to be over an hour trip to get where we're going, and we're going to want to be rested when we get there, if at all possible."

June admittedly knew very little about submarines. The sum total of her knowledge on the subject had come from seeing *Das Boot* in a film class in college and from a documentary about Jacques Cousteau on Disney Plus. Neither prepared her in the slightest for the vessel they were currently in. She highly doubted this was even the kind of submarine the military would use. Instead it looked almost like a one-of-a-kind custom job intended less to emulate military or research craft and instead act more like an underwater pleasure yacht. Maury carefully guided her through an empty hallway lined in expensive woods that June couldn't hope to identify, then through a non-obtrusive door into a much tighter hallway that June would guess was for servants and crew. There were several voices coming from one end of the hall. Maury pointed her in the opposite direction until they reached a small store room full of maintenance equipment. Along the way June noticed multiple security cameras, although none of them had lights on that would indicate they were functioning. Once Maury shut the door behind them, that was the first thing she addressed.

"Is anyone on this thing's security team going to check the video feeds and realize we're here?"

"Not right now, no," he said. "I bribed one of the security guys to stop the recording for about a ten minute time frame. I kind of led them to believe that I wanted to smuggle some pot to where we're going, and if they did this for me I would be their hookup."

"And is that something you can actually get for them?"

"No, and I think eventually they might start to get suspicious, but it was the best I could come up with on short notice. I couldn't think of any other way to smuggle you on here so you can see what's going on."

"So what *is* going on? Because so far all I've got from you is some unlikely hints about theme parks.

Honestly, that doesn't sound at all like a reason for Logane to go to this level of secrecy."

"There's a lot more to it than anyone on the conspiracy websites have figured out."

June reached into her purse to pull out her phone to record the conversation, but Maury put his hand over hers to stop her.

"No recording me," he said. "I'm already pushing myself into dangerous territory without having my voice on record as the one giving you all this info."

"I need to have something tangible to bring back with me," June said. "Something to show that I at least am not the one making this up."

"Trust me, you'll have a lot very soon," Maury said. "You may want to keep your smartphone ready when we get there. You're going to want pictures."

"Can I at least take notes as you talk?"

"Sure. I guess." Maury found a nearby tool bench to sit on. June sat on the floor across from him, making sure she was in a position to see his face and his expressions the whole time.

"First, if you don't want to say anything about your identity," June said, "can you at least give me some idea how you have access to all of this?"

"I guess you can call me an independent contractor," Maury said. "That's vague enough. I was recruited and hired on to help work on something, but I was forced to sign a strict NDA."

"And I assume that talking to me now is a violation of that?" June asked.

"And then some. I needed the work, and I've worked some shady jobs before. I guess maybe I'd developed a reputation for keeping my mouth shut. But I can't keep my mouth shut about what I've seen."

Maury went quiet. June almost asked him a question, but she had the impression that he would be more than willing to spill plenty of details without her prompting if she just kept silent and let him get whatever was going on off his chest.

Finally, Maury spoke again. "You see, people have died. Other contractors working on other parts of the project. At first I thought it was just an accident here or there, people not being careful where they should have been. But now after what I've seen... uh, I don't think they were all accidents. I think some of the deaths were very much intentional. To keep some people silent."

June sat up straight on the floor. "Are you sure about that?"

"No. Not quite," Maury said. "But once you see what this is all about, you'll understand."

"All of this for some kind of underwater theme park," June said. "No, I can't say I think it will be likely that I will understand."

"Well, that's why I needed to bring someone down to actually see Trenchland with their own eyes. If I try to just tell anyone what I've seen, no one would believe me."

"So are you going to tell me what you've seen or not?" June said.

"No. I told you, you have to see it for yourself. If I tell you now, you won't really understand and might try to do something ill-advised."

"So then tell me exactly what you're planning to happen here tonight, then," June said. "You can say that much, at least, right?"

"Look, I can't disappear for too long at a time, but I can hide you in certain places like this where there aren't any cameras. When I can vanish from what I'm supposed to be doing, and when I can be sure cameras are either looking away or turned off, I can lead or direct you to the places and things that you're going to want to see to get your whole story. And trust me, there's a lot here. You trust me on that part at least, right? That just what little you've seen so far is enough to tell you that something huge is happening?"

"Yeah, I suppose. But exactly how huge are we talking?"

"Huge in every sense. Figuratively, you're going to see things that will change how you think of science and the world at large. Literally, in that what I've got to show you is going to be physically massive."

June resisted an intense urge to say "That's what she said." That would hardly be helpful right now.

"Okay, so if you can't tell me exactly what's going on, or you don't think I'll believe it without seeing, then what can you tell me?"

"I can tell you that I have a thumb drive hidden in my locker at our destination," Maury said. "You're going to want to get as much evidence for yourself as you can, but for things you won't just be able to snap pictures of, the thumb drive will help."

"What kind of things?"

"Financial records, mostly. A few pieces of info showing how Logane was able to get Trenchland built without it showing up on anyone's radar. And… a couple of bits of evidence that he might have engaged in foul play to cover certain things up."

June looked down at her hands in her lap and thought about all this. The way evidence in this case had so often seemed to dry up so quickly, she had often wondered if Logane might be up to something insidious. Maury's words seemed to suggest that she had been right. It was all the more reason to be careful. If Logane really was capable of such a thing, he wouldn't have any qualms about going to extremes to keep a reporter quiet.

"You've already said Trenchland is some kind of underwater theme park," June said. "That's crazy as hell, but not the sort of thing you would expect anyone to kill to keep a secret. Especially since it would eventually be open to the public anyway, right?"

"Yes and no. It is supposed to be public eventually. But what he's done here, it's beyond anything anyone has ever created before."

"In what way?"

"You won't believe it unless…"

"Unless I see it. Right. You said that already."

"And I'm going to keep saying it. Because I'm not exaggerating."

"Fine. Whatever. What about this: you said you were an independent contractor hired for this. What kind of contractor? What have you specifically been doing as a part of this?"

"I've been leading one of the teams building parts of the underwater structure," Maury said. "There were a number of teams, many of them unaware of what the other teams were specifically working on in order to hide certain facts about what it all meant. Logane, I think, didn't want anyone to realize the full extent of what we were building. But

I put together enough rumors that I was able to know where to look when I was snooping, and I finally saw enough things I wasn't supposed to see. That's when I began looking for someone like you to help reveal to everyone else what was going on."

"Are you sure you can't give me any more hints?" June asked. "Any at all? Anything to make me not think that I'm wasting my time?"

Maury shook his head. "You are definitely not wasting your time."

That was about the end of their conversation for the rest of the trip.

CHAPTER THREE

Maury was right that the trip took roughly an hour, and it was a long hour indeed. It consisted mostly of the two of them sitting in awkward silence in the maintenance room, punctuated occasionally by June trying to get more info out of Maury and Maury constantly repeating "you just have to see it for yourself." At the very least, June was able to get a few personal details out of Maury, not that she would be able to use them in anything she wrote if she really wanted to keep his identity a secret. Apparently he was originally from Montana, had no real family left alive to speak of, and had been doing the same job for most of his life. He gave up very little about what kind of contracting work he had done in the past. He would only say that he had worked on structures for powerful people who wouldn't take kindly to that knowledge being shared with anyone. He did let slip that at least one of those people may have been a powerful mob boss, and also that he may or may not have worked on a large doomsday bunker for a certain very rich and very paranoid celebrity. After that, all conversation dried up.

Eventually, through some kind of sign that only Maury could apparently notice, the sub started its preparations to dock with wherever they were going, and Maury told her to get up and be ready to follow his lead in exiting. June had no earthly idea on where they might be under the surface, but she was pretty sure that they hadn't gone up at any time. The name of their destination suggested it was in some trench, of course, but June's knowledge of Earth's underwater cartography was practically nil, so that wasn't a solid clue for now. Vaguely she wondered what exactly she was supposed to do if something went wrong and she ended up trapped deep in the ocean, but she tried to tell herself that Maury wouldn't have led her here if he didn't have some kind of escape route ready. She just had no idea what it could possibly be.

"Once the sub docks, we'll have a limited window to get out before anyone else sees us. Everyone on the inside will be too busy trying to make sure the docking has finished properly, and there's next to no one on the outside monitoring anything. All of Trenchland is still on a skeleton crew at this point. So when I say so, we'll have to move fast back in the direction we originally came. And we can't dawdle, or else we're in serious danger. Understand?"

June wasn't entirely sure that she did understand, not completely. She understood, of course, that messing around in the secrets of one of the richest men in the world was always extremely risky, but was this risky like she could lose her job and livelihood, or risky like she could lose her life? In the end she decided she wasn't quite ready to know yet, so instead she just nodded in Maury's direction.

Getting back up to the main submarine entrance was easy enough, although she wasn't sure how much she believed they could exit without anyone seeing them at all. Despite what Maury said, there had to be someone around, right? Yet once the door opened she found herself in a room very much like the one they had left earlier, something that looked like an enormous warehouse with a pool in the center for subs to come and go. The most obvious difference was that, while the warehouse they had left was fairly run-down looking, this place was slick and new, all shining metal and polymer walls with not a single hint of grime to them yet.

"You said we're underwater," June said as Maury led her to a dark corner with a large stack of crates. "Just exactly how far underwater? With a name like Trenchland... I mean, we can't actually be in the Mariana Trench, can we?"

"There's more than one trench in the ocean, Miss Reilly," Maury said. "Although I think part of the idea of the name is to make any tourists think that the trench we're in is in fact that fabled deepest part of the ocean. But the engineering required to build an entire theme park underwater was already cost-prohibitive, even with Mr. Logane spending more money on it than any non-billionaire will ever witness in their entire lifetime."

Maury stopped her in a nook between several crates and a number of shelves full of what looked like high-tech engine parts. From the outside June doubted anyone would be able to see them, but it still provided a good view of most of the docking arena. "Okay, so can you finally give me some idea of what's going on here?" June asked. "I've heard many conspiracy theories about what Logane is doing while he's been disappeared, but not a single one of them had anything to do with an underwater theme park. It doesn't seem like the kind of thing he'd want to hide. He'd want the world to know about it so he could show off, show everyone how clever he is and how much money he has to blow on a random whim."

"Yeah, that's part of the problem," Maury said. He looked at a watch on his wrist and hissed. "Crap.

We don't have much time left before I have to be somewhere, so I'm going to go over what I can as quickly and succinctly as possible. Just listen, and if you have any questions I can answer them later. Got it?"

June nodded as she pulled out her phone and began recording.

"A couple of years before Logane fell off the radar, a lot of people who worked in higher end construction and engineering started going missing. The word was that someone with a lot of money was putting together something big that they didn't want anyone else to know about right away, and they were willing to pay extreme money to get people to do the work and keep quiet about it for a while. Then some guy came along and confirmed that, offered me a deal to be part of the crew down here. Yeah, I know that's sketchy as hell, but once I realized who the money was I actually thought that made it more legitimate, you know? I mean, Dom Logane is a household name that could buy pretty much any giant company he wanted to in the world. If he's doing something big, it will be in the news eventually and I figured it would only be a matter of time before I wouldn't have to keep it a secret anymore."

"Except that's not the case anymore, I take it?" June asked.

"Just let me get this out, okay? No interrupting. So everything was good and I was really proud of what we were doing down here, but it was all very compartmentalized. No one really knew one hundred percent about what this place was supposed to be. Until they started bringing in Trenchland's so-called attractions. That's when a lot of the people working down here started to realize we were in over our heads."

June really wanted to ask what exactly these "attractions" were supposed to be, but Maury didn't look like he would appreciate any more questions just yet. So she just nodded and made damn sure that the phone kept recording.

"So I started keeping track of a few things I wasn't supposed to, gathering little bits of information here and there. I have it all on a thumb drive hidden in my locker. Forty-six, thirty-two, seven. Add it to everything I'm going to be able to show you tonight, and I think it points to something way bigger than anyone ever thought. And right about the time I started to get my suspicions up about what might actually be happening here, I started losing contact with a few of the people around here. I think... I think Logane might have quietly had them removed."

June's jaw dropped open, and this time she couldn't keep herself from speaking. "Removed? Removed as in the way I think you're saying?"

"I think so, although I don't have any proof of that part yet." Maury looked at his watch again. "Listen to me. I have to go meet with someone quickly. I'm going to leave you hidden here, and once I come back I'll start taking you around to the attractions."

"Wait, what? You can't just…"

"It's just a mandatory daily staff meeting, and it's going to be right over there." Maury pointed to a spot further down the docks from the sub that had brought them here. "That's why I'm hiding you right here. It's got a clear view of where I'll be and you'll be able to see me the whole time, but no one will be able to see you as long as you don't make any noise."

"Maury, no, I don't feel like…"

"Five, ten minutes tops. Just stay quiet no matter what, got it?"

Maury didn't give her a chance to respond. He was away from the hiding spot and walking toward his upcoming meeting before June could give any further objection.

June watched from her hiding spot while other people started to filter in and join Maury. Most of them were dressed like construction workers or were in jumpsuits, while one or two were in slightly nicer clothes, likely some kind of foremen or middle management. There were about ten in all, and all of them milled about chatting with each other. Nothing in their demeanor suggested this was anything other than a routine meeting, at least for the first minute or so. Then June saw a ripple of nervousness grow through the crowd, and one by one each of them came to stare in one particular direction. June followed their gaze to see six armed men come through a side door, followed close behind by the man, the myth, the legend, Dom Logane himself.

Everyone and their grandmother had seen pictures and videos of Dom Logane at some point, but it was another thing entirely for June to finally see him in real life, even if she couldn't honestly say it was face to face yet. Maybe that time would be in the near future, and maybe she would even be able to get a few answers out of him, although she doubted he would ever answer honestly to some lowly reporter like herself. For now she would simply have to look and watch carefully while he didn't know he was being observed. Any little detail she could bring back with her to the surface may be something important when she finally broke this story to the rest of the world. He was in what looked like the exact same suit he wore for all his press release photos, a look which included no tie and the first several buttons on his expensive white silk shirt unbuttoned. The man was in his sixties but hid it well, especially here in reality where he looked like he might actually be a very fit man in his forties. At one point he had been listed in People Magazine as one of their sexiest men of the year, and even now she could still see it. But even with that, there was something cold and calculating about him, like he was aware of every single step or swing of his arms and what it said about him.

The same could not be said of the men with him. These were people of brute force, each of them wearing tactical gear and carrying very large guns. Although June had never seen their like in real life, she could only look at them and assume they were hired mercenaries of some sort, and highly efficient and expensive ones at that. One of them seemed to be the leader, but the rest of them all blended together as to be unrecognizable from one another.

Logane stopped in front of the group that was about to have their meeting, and although June couldn't believe it, she was already sure she knew exactly what was about to happen.

Although there was some distance between her and the two groups, she was still able to make out what Logane said when he spoke.

"Ladies and gentlemen, I want to thank you for all the work you've done for me over the past... aw hell. Screw it. I'm not in the mood for the speech right now. Caslaw, just get it over with so we can get on to the next group."

As one, all of the mercs raised their weapons at Maury and his group. None of them had a chance to get out even a single word of protest before the gunfire started.

CHAPTER FOUR

As a reporter, June had seen horrible things before. She'd been at the scene of mass shootings and attacks, so she had seen dead bodies on a larger scale. But this was the first time she had ever witnessed multiple murders in real time.

Her first instinct of course was to scream, but her second instinct thankfully was to bring her hands up and cover her mouth. Maury had specifically said that she wouldn't be found if she didn't make any noise. Later this would make her wonder if maybe this meant he had known or suspected this was going to happen. For now, though, she wasn't capable of that kind of analysis. She could only watch in stunned horror as the bullets ripped through the flesh of Maury and his coworkers.

Although it lasted forever in her mind, in reality the slaughter only took a handful of seconds. The mercs were efficient, with no bullets wasted and their targets down from head or chest shots before most of the victims would have even understood what was happening to them.

As the last gunshots echoed through the cavernous room, June could see Logane saying a few words to the mercs, although she couldn't hear any of what he said. Then he turned and walked right back through the same door he'd come out of. One of the mercs, someone June could only assume was the leader, pointed to two of his people and gave them orders. He and the other three guards followed Logane through the door, while the remaining two set down their weapons and began gathering the bodies.

June ducked down behind the crate, keeping her hand on her mouth the whole time just in case she unwittingly made some squeak that gave away her position. Her brain was locked up, trying to deny what she had just seen. The hand over her mouth suddenly felt wet, and she realized she was crying. She hadn't known Maury for more than a few hours, but that didn't make it easier to see him gunned down in cold blood. She had no idea who the others had all been, but likely somewhere there would be family and friends that would never see them again, and never have any answers as to what had happened.

And right now, June didn't really have any answers either. She had been expecting major secrets tonight, but she hadn't quite been ready for them to be the kind someone was willing to kill over. All of this over a theme park? That didn't make any sense at all.

She allowed herself a couple of minutes to catch her breath, listening carefully the whole time just in case footsteps started heading in the direction of her position. So far she had no reason to believe anyone other than Maury had realized she was here, so she was probably safe in that regard, but without Maury she had no idea how to leave. And she didn't even have any evidence of what she had just seen...

Wait. Actually, she realized, she did have at least some. She looked at her hands, then frantically searched her pockets, and found nothing. There was a brief moment of panic before she thought to look around her. Finally she saw it, her cell phone, on the floor about a foot away from her. She must have dropped it when she put her hands over her mouth. She scrambled to grab it, then checked to make sure it hadn't broken in the fall. When she was satisfied it still worked, she checked on the recording she had been making of Maury's words.

It had stopped recording at some point, most likely when she had dropped it. And she could check to make sure, not while there were still people in the docking room that might hear it, but she was pretty sure she hadn't turned off the recording when Maury had left for the meeting. It had still been recording all the way through the gunshots. That wasn't the hardest of evidence, but it was a start.

And there's more, June thought. Maury had said he had a thumb drive hidden in his locker. If she could find that, she would be able to prove to the rest of the world that something horrible was going on here.

And then she just needed to figure out how to get back to the surface without dying. As much as she wanted to worry about that, she forced herself to compartmentalize her mind in order to keep going. One task at a time. After she got the thumb drive, then she would figure out her next move.

So the first thing she was going to need to do if she wanted to survive was to get some sense of where she was in relation to where she wanted to go. She peeked up around the crates again, thinking she might take just a moment to get some shots or video of the mercs cleaning up the bodies, but either she had taken longer to get her head together than she thought or the mercs were very good at their jobs. Both the bodies and the mercs were gone, although there was still blood pooled on the floor. She took a couple of snapshots of that, then started searching for some nearby door she could sneak through.

She didn't have to search for long, as the quickest path out of here ended up being the most obvious one. The area was designed to receive visitors, after all, and lead them on through into the theme park proper. There was a large arched doorway, although any signage that was supposed to go over the top to announce the theme park's name was not in place yet. The area past it was open and bare, probably with the intention of having this whole part full of kiosks and souvenir stands. June made sure to keep to the shadowy corners of the room, which was easier since a lot of lighting for the area either hadn't been installed yet or was turned off.

At the far end of the room there was an enormous glass window looking out into a deep, dark tank of water that by itself was probably big enough to contain two or three football fields. Despite herself, June stopped in front of it. While she had much more important things to worry about right now, her mind finally came back to the question that had been plaguing her since she'd first heard Maury call this place Trenchland. Just what exactly was the point of a theme park deep under the ocean? What were the attractions?

This tank obviously had to be where one of the attractions went, the first big show any tourists would get upon entering the park, but at this exact second she couldn't see anything in the tank that would warrant any awe. The water was dark and deep and murky. She had to squint at first, but the longer she stared the more she thought she saw something moving out in the water.

It only took a second for the creature in the water to rush out of the gloom and come at the glass. Something fish-like, something huge beyond her easy understanding. It turned away from hitting the glass at the last moment, giving her a clear view of the monstrosity in profile. It was a shark. Or, at least, what a shark might look like if it were large enough to bite a submarine in half.

Every fiber of June's being told her to run, even though that of course didn't make sense. There were four to six inches worth of glass and millions of gallons of water between her and the prehistoric nightmare in the aquarium, but logic was nowhere near enough to calm the rising panic in her.

The creature in the enclosure, however, barely seemed to notice or care that she existed, at least for the moment. Maybe it was smart enough to know that it couldn't get at anything on this side of the glass, or maybe even she was too small for this gargantuan thing to even consider her as worthy prey. As her initial terror started to subside, the thinking part of June's brain started to piece together all the little bits and pieces of knowledge that she'd picked up from movies and college science classes in an attempt to identify what, exactly, she may be looking at. Her first frame of reference, of course was the movie *Jaws*, which might lead her to believe this was indeed some variation of a great white shark like she had initially thought. But even that mechanical puppet from the movie was like a minnow compared to this. From snout to tail, she thought this thing might actually be as long as a short train. It was incredibly pale, with dark eyes each larger than her head. It swam languidly past her place at the glass, its enormous tail going back and forth probably with enough force to smash her into a bloody pulp if she were to get in the way of it.

Megalodon, she finally remembered. That was the name of what this thing reminded her off. Some kind of giant prehistoric shark. There was no way something like this should be alive, and yet somehow here it was, swimming in front of her as though it had every right to be in this place and epoch.

June backed away from the glass and deeper into the shadows of the hall. This had to be it. This had to be the secret that Logane had been keeping for the last couple of years, the secret he had been willing to kill Maury for, as well as an unknown number of others. He had a creature in his possession that wasn't supposed to exist, and he wanted to keep it a secret.

But even as June thought that, she realized it couldn't possibly be the whole truth. Just from what little she had seen of the Trenchland complex so far, it was far bigger than was needed to sustain this single enormous tank and its occupant. Was it possible that Logane had more than one of these megalodon things? Or even other such creatures that shouldn't exist any longer in the world? Yes, she suspected that had to be the case. If Trenchland was indeed intended as a theme park, then there was no way it could all be based on a single attraction.

What else was it possible to have in here? What else could be so enormous and terrifying and in defiance of known modern science that Dom Logane would be willing to kill so many people in order to keep it a secret? And why even keep it a secret for so long anyway? This place obviously intended to be opened to a paying public at some point, so it couldn't be considered a secret worth killing for.

Unless there was more here, things that *wouldn't* be seen by the public.

That thought by itself was enough to rouse her from any paralysis and fear that had been coursing through her from the moment she'd seen Logane order the murder of his own people. She was a reporter, after all, and there was an incredible amount here to report. The megalodon alone would be enough to write the defining story of her career. But there was more. Maybe more dark secrets, things she couldn't comprehend yet, or maybe just more fantastical creatures of the deep. Either way, it was time for her to get moving. There were sights and sounds in Trenchland for her to record and see, as well as an escape to plan. Because she could get all the pictures and video she wanted, and it still wouldn't ensure her survival down here.

With her thoughts starting to follow a more logical, less frenzied path, June finally thought to take out her smart phone. Maury had said from the beginning that there would be things she'd want to record, and here was a big one swimming around right in front of her. She aimed the phone at the glass and took about a minute of footage, doing her best to make it as clear as possible even as the megalodon swam far enough away in its enclosure that she couldn't be sure it would be enough to convince anyone. She could stick around and try to record it for longer, but she had a feeling it wouldn't be wise to stay in place for too long, and that she would need to save some space on the phone for many other videos to come.

Although she doubted it would do her any good, she tried for a moment to see if she could download the video to the cloud from here. Predictably, it was hard to get a decent cell or wi-fi signal from hundreds of feet below the water. So none of this information would get out if she didn't get out as well.

June gave one last look at the Megalodon, then began her search for the employee locker room.

CHAPTER FIVE

It didn't take her too long to find a door that was obviously intended for employees only, even if there still wasn't any signage up indicating that. There was a keypad next to the door that gave June pause, but when she tried the door it opened for her. That made a little bit of sense, she supposed. A lot of the security measures meant to keep guests out of the back areas wouldn't need to be working yet when the employees were still the only people that even knew this place existed.

Beyond the door, the hallway was a long passage of concrete, plastic, and metal that went off in either direction, with occasional doors breaking up the monotony of the spartan space. There wasn't any official signage up back here either that would direct employees to the various places they needed to go, but someone with a piece of paper and a Sharpie had taped some hand-made directions with arrows to the wall just across from the door. Following that, it didn't take her long to find a break room and locker room beyond it. She was cautious as she looked inside, half expecting employees to be milling about, but there was no one. Maybe the only employees that had been here were now among the bodies gathered by the mercs, or maybe she was just here at a time when no one would be around. That made her wonder how many employees were actually currently in the complex, and just how many were being or about to be executed for the same mysterious reasons as Maury and the others. Whatever the answer, she didn't think it was a good idea to stick around in one spot for too long. She needed to get in here, see if Maury's locker had what she needed, and then get to some place less conspicuous.

The locker room was too new to have developed the standard funk she associated with such places, but it had definitely been in use up until recently. About a third of the lockers had new combination locks on them, each of them with a piece of tape with a hastily scrawled name on it indicating who each one belonged to. It suddenly occurred to her that she might be in trouble if the names were all surnames, since she had never gotten the chance to get Maury's last name out of him. Most of them, thankfully, seemed to have first names with last initials on tape, and June carefully went down the row until she found one marked "Maury J." She found herself stuck, though, when she saw the lock on the handle. In the past she had found it useful to know how to pick locks in her line of business, but a combination lock was a different matter entirely. If it was possible to listen to it and hear the tumblers in place, that was a skill she had never learned.

For a moment June worried that she'd come all this way to be stopped by a single metal lock, and she started to wonder if there was something around her that she might use to break the lock open while still somehow not alerting anyone to her presence. It was too bad that…

June stopped what she was doing and thought back to the brief conversation she'd had with Maury just before his shocking demise. He'd been adamant that she not interrupt him, but there had been something he'd said around the point where he was talking about the thumb drive, something that had seemed almost nonsensical, that she would have asked for clarification on if she'd had the chance. While she couldn't remember exactly what it had been, she didn't have to remember. She took out her phone and pulled up the recording she'd made of him talking. June double checked to make sure there was no indication that anyone was coming or that there were any cameras in the room, then played the recording and re-listened to the first half of it. Honestly she didn't want to listen to what was in the second half again, but she shouldn't have to.

"…started keeping track of a few things I wasn't supposed to, gathering little bits of information here and there. I have it all on a thumb drive hidden in my locker. Forty-six, thirty-two, seven. Add it to everything…"

Right there. The random numbers he'd said after mentioning his locker. It had to be the combination. But why would he have casually added that into the conversation? It didn't make any sense.

Unless, June suddenly realized, he had known or at least half-suspected he wouldn't be around when she went for the thumb drive. Had he known he was about to be killed? He couldn't have been sure, or else he wouldn't have causally walked over to what he said was supposed to be a routine meeting. But given his suspicions about everything else, he may have decided to give that little tidbit to her just in case. And she was very glad he had.

"Sorry, Maury," she muttered as she spun the dial to each number. The tumbler on the lock clicked into place, and June silently said a prayer of thanks as she took the lock off and opened the locker. The first things she saw inside were a number of work jumpsuits, a few of them stained with dirt or grease. Apparently the work Maury had done hadn't just been supervisory in nature. He'd had to get deep into the workings of things in order to build or repair. June paused as an idea occurred to her. It might be in her best interest to put one of these on. While a lot of the security didn't seem to be fully operational yet, or at least was not monitored as much as it could be, it would be much better if she looked like she belonged here in the event that someone accidentally came across her. Of course, given what she had seen done to Maury and the others, there was no actual guarantee of safety even if any believed she actually belonged here. But it was better than nothing.

She immediately put on a pair of overalls, trying to ignore the body odor smell wafting off of them the whole time. There was also a security badge with Maury's face and name on it. Apparently his full name had been Maury Jacobson. She debated for a moment whether she wanted to add that to her outfit. Would it still work to get her into anyplace Maury had been allowed before, or would it already have been deactivated? She decided she had to risk it. Hopefully no one had decided that deactivating the badge was a priority for someone who obviously couldn't use it anymore. It would be a problem if someone looked closely at it and realized she wasn't the older man pictured, but she rubbed her finger in some of the grease on her overalls, then smeared it over the picture. It wouldn't fool anyone who took a really close look, but it might at least buy her a little bit of time at some point.

Hell, it might not even matter. Half the security measures in this place didn't seem to be online yet anyway.

Now that she had something vaguely resembling camouflage, she figured she finally had a moment to stop and gain her bearings. It occurred to her that she was incredibly hungry, and she took a moment to rummage through the random items in Maury's locker hoping for some kind of snack. There was a half-finished bag of M&Ms in one of the jumpsuit pockets, and although that wasn't the most appetizing option right now, it was at least a quick source of sugar and energy. As she ate the partially melted candies, she took a moment to look around the rest of the locker room. It was large enough to accommodate many more employees than she had seen so far, but only a small number of the lockers appeared to be in use. The rest were new and freshly painted just like the rest of Trenchland. So that could only mean that at some point, the theme park really was intended to require a normal-sized workforce. A workforce, she now assumed, that wouldn't have been witness to things that may have occurred here before it had opened.

So what all needed to be concealed? It couldn't just be the megalodon and, she assumed, any other such prehistoric creatures here. Even workplace accidents like someone accidentally falling into a monster's tank and getting eaten could have probably been swept under the rug without needing to go to the extremes she had seen so far.

June was so frazzled and stuck in her own thoughts that she almost walked away without looking for the thumb drive. After digging around on the bottom of the locker for a bit she found it shoved behind a pair of grungy work boots. If she could find some kind of computer she could put this in, she might be able to go over the files inside and get a better idea of what else she might be looking for. Or there might be more information elsewhere, something like videos. Maybe there was a security station that had footage of what had happened to Maury and the others. After all, she had the sound of gunshots on her phone and footage of the aftermath, but if she could get video of the actual execution that would be much more of a nail in Dom Logane's coffin.

With those two possible paths before her, June had a plan of action but still no plan of escape. That was very worrying, but maybe an answer would present itself as she saw more of what the mysterious Trenchland had to offer. And she wouldn't see any of that if she stayed in place. So, with a deep breath and a heavy effort to block out some of the traumatic images that still flashed in front of her eyes, June quietly left the locker room and began the search for more of the story.

CHAPTER SIX

There were no hand-made signs indicating where in the back halls the security station might be, so June found her way into the main halls and, from there, found herself with so many directions she could go that she was at a loss. While most of the spaces on the wall for signs were still bare, a few had already been put up and directed her down the halls to what June could only assume were the names of other sea creatures that weren't supposed to exist. A couple of them were scientific sounding names that she assumed had to belong to creatures that were supposed to be long extinct. Those all seemed to be in the same direction. In a different direction, signs suggested names that June recognized as being from myths and folklore. Kraken, Selkie, Fiji Mermaid. That last one gave her pause. She remembered it from pop culture, maybe some old X-Files episode if she was remembering it correctly. The Fiji Mermaid had been a side-show attraction created by

P.T. Barnum by sewing the torso of a dead monkey onto the tail of a fish. Pretty much no culture had ever believed it was a real thing. So if it had never actually existed like the megalodon, how could Logane possibly have one to display in Trenchland?

Maybe he had created it in a lab. Maybe everything here had been created in a lab. She'd almost thought that the megalodon might have been discovered in the wild, but this suggested otherwise.

If Logane had the genetics technology to create things like this, what else could he create? How could that tech be used in the outside world? For military technology?

June was beginning to see why he might be willing to kill to keep a few of his secrets.

She hesitated, looking at some of the signs. She desperately wanted to see what some of these things looked like, and she was sure that recordings of them would be helpful to her cause. But video alone wasn't enough. Video could be altered, especially in the era of deep fakes and AI art. She needed more evidence than just that. So there had to be somewhere else she could go that would get her things she needed.

She thought again about the security station, but from here she wasn't sure where that might be. This whole complex was huge. She could run around for hours and not find what she needed. Briefly she wondered if maybe she could look for the nearest security camera and follow some wires from it back to a central point, but that was her thinking like she was in some ridiculous old movie. Modern cameras didn't need to be wired directly to any monitor.

She looked again at the various signs in front of her. Mosasaurus, plesiosaurus, shastasaurus, information kiosk, Charybdis, Leviathan...

Wait. Maybe she was way overthinking this. This was supposed to be a theme park in the end, after all. With little other choice, she started off in the direction of the information kiosk.

Even though she felt time was of the essence, she really felt that she had no choice but to stop every hundred feet or so as a new enclosure became visible to her, usually with what appeared to be nothing but deep blue water beyond. Yet more often than not, if she stared into the deep for long enough she would catch a hint of something beyond. Most of the time that was all it was, a hint: a flipper, the end of a tail, a barely seen flash of what could have been teeth. Most of those tanks didn't yield anything she could record in the half minute or so that she stood there.

But every so often, something would be right up front for her to see. They were often very fast and again didn't result in any clear footage. Some, however, were more photogenic and swam around in their enclosures slow enough and close enough to the glass that she was able to get very clear video. One looked very similar to what she assumed the Loch Ness Monster would look like, with a long neck and a small head that nonetheless had a mouth full of sharp teeth that would still be able to rip apart anyone that ended up in the water with it. Whether or not it was actually supposed to be Nessie or if it was some prehistoric creature she couldn't quite name, she had no way of knowing. Most of the tanks didn't have signage. Some had signage with cryptic or terrifying names like Mauisaurus or kaiju Shark, but with no sign whatsoever that anything inhabited the tanks.

In one tank, something that looked like a more reptilian version of a blue whale came up very close to the glass and looked at her with big, soulful eyes that shined with intelligence, and while she couldn't be sure, she thought it might have actually tried to wave at her with one of its flippers before lazily swimming away.

Another tank had both signage and an occupant, June had trouble believing what she was seeing. The creature was labeled as Charybdis, which she knew from old college lit classes as one of the fearsome sea monsters Odysseus had run across in Homer's The Odyssey. The creature's MO was to suck down unsuspecting sailors through a whirlpool, but in most interpretations of the mythology the creature was never seen. It was just a mouth in the water. Now here, right in front of her, was something which very well could have been the monster of legend, or it could have been something else entirely that the powers that be of Trenchland just named after it. The closest thing June could compare it to with her minimal knowledge of marine biology was an anglerfish, given that it had a hinged jaw that would open far wider even than its actual head, but that was about where the similarities stopped. This thing didn't have the glowing antenna that she associated with that deep sea fish, nor was it anywhere even in the ballpark of the same size. The tank that held it was maybe slightly smaller than the one that had held the megalodon, but this thing took up almost the entire space. June would have thought it was a bad idea to keep something so big in a relatively tiny enclosure, except it didn't swim or move or in any way mind that it didn't have a lot of room around it. It simply sat in the middle of the tank, its giant maw open and pointed directly above it, where June thought there might be more rooms for people or caretakers to walk over the specimens. The creature's massive fins only moved enough to keep it from floating away from its spot. From the perspective of any keepers feeding it from above, it probably did just look like a huge whirlpool from which nothing would ever come out.

A few windows down, in an area that was mostly dark with no signs and barely any acknowledgement at all that there was anything here, the glass looked out into a deep, black hole beneath the complex. The only thing that could be seen in it were a few shadowy tendrils, possibly tentacles, waving in the depths like giant stalks of seaweed. Or, maybe, like the feelers of something unfathomable that was just waiting for something to come too close before it revealed itself. June rushed past that one, and did her best not to consider what may or may not be down there.

At the end of one row there was a display on the wall marked "The Fiji Mermaid," and at first June thought that her earlier questions about how something like that could exist had the most obvious of all possible answers, that it actually didn't. It was mounted on the wall instead of a live exhibit, and here at least the signage appeared mostly complete. There was a board next to it explaining the historical significance, including info about P. T. Barnum and what he had done to fake the Mermaid's existence. Logane must have gotten ahold of the original Fiji Mermaid at some point or made a facsimile.

Except when June got closer, she realized there was no way this could be the original mummified monkey and fish combo. Because the one mounted on the display looked fresh, like it had only recently been taxidermized and put together. And there was no obvious line where the dead monkey ended and the dead fish began. In fact, if June didn't know any better, she would say it looked suspiciously like it *really was* a half-monkey, half-fish creature, and it had been taxidermized and displayed as if it was fake.

Just what the hell was with this place? None of it made much sense to her.

Ignoring the uneasy feelings that the fake/non-fake Fiji Mermaid gave her, June finally found her way to a kiosk that looked like it was designed for information. Unfortunately for her, there was no signage here, so her hope that she could find something here pointing her in the direction of security looked like it was for nothing. She almost didn't look any further, but on a whim she decided to actually get behind the information desk and see if there would be anything useful. Under the desk she found a box, and on it was a memo, something about everything inside needing to be returned to the printer before some supervisor named "Joanie" found out that these had been ordered before it was authorized. June thought there would be a story there, maybe even a clue as to what may or may not really be going on here, but any idea about deciphering it went away when she opened the box's flaps and saw what was inside.

Theme park maps. The box was full of freshly printed theme park maps. June grabbed one off the top and opened it up. The map wasn't intended to be completely accurate. It was done in a cartoony style with an anthropomorphic megalodon smiler at the map's holder and pointing out places of interest. But despite emphasizing design over accuracy, it did at least show the general locations of things like bathrooms, snack stands, guest lockers, and, yes, security.

"Thank you," June said quietly. "Thank you, uh…" She looked at the label underneath the cartoon megalodon, "Meggie. I never thought I would be so grateful for a cartoon fish."

She looked over the map again, identified roughly where she currently was based on what attractions she had already passed, then determined the general direction she had to go. She almost set the souvenir map back down in the box, then thought better of it. It was hardly something she wanted to bet her life on if it came down to that, but the rough general directions might still be useful to her in the near future.

The security station shouldn't be far from here. Maybe all of this was almost over.

CHAPTER SEVEN

It wasn't. She got lost several times over the next twenty minutes before she finally found a door down a side hall with a hand-written sign on it that said "Security." Up until this point she had found little to no evidence that there was anyone else in the many places she had searched so far, as though the people killed at the docks really were the only people who'd actually been in the entire complex. That obviously couldn't be true, of course, since even incomplete, a facility of this size had to have more people around somewhere to run it. Now, finally, as she carefully approached the security door, she was getting that evidence. From inside she could hear music playing, some sort of 70's era arena rock, the kind of music that immediately made June think whoever was beyond the door had to be a pudgy white guy in his forties or fifties. She supposed it was possible that there was more than one person in here, but given the ghost town nature of the rest of the place, she somehow doubted it. Still, regardless of how many people were inside, she was going to approach the situation as if it were dangerous. Before she came any closer to the door, she pulled her gun out of her purse and made sure it was loaded.

She had to pause as she held the gun in her hand. She'd fired it plenty of times on the practice range, and once or twice when she had been out in the field reporting she had felt intimidated enough that she'd considered drawing the weapon, but this was the first time she thought she might very well need to fire it at a person before the day was over. If she was lucky that wouldn't be needed at all here in this exact moment, but when there was apparently a mercenary death squad roaming the premises that had already shown itself fully capable of performing unthinking executions, she completely expected that she would fire it before she left this place.

If she was able to leave Trenchland at all, of course.

With the gun drawn yet not pointed at anything other than the floor, she slowly and carefully tried the handle of the door. Like most of the back rooms in this place so far, this one had a security keypad that didn't seem wired up or turned on yet. She raised her weapon as the door swung open, but so far there didn't appear to be anyone on the other side. This particular room was an office with a couple of desks, but only one of them had anything on it. There were a few papers and a vape pen next to a Bluetooth speaker that was blaring the music. There were some filing cabinets that June was willing to guess were empty, and the walls were bare of any pictures or posters that might normally appear in an office that someone had occupied for some time. There were three other doors, one of which was marked as a bathroom, but only one of them was slightly ajar. The room beyond was mostly dark but had the flicker and glow of screens or monitors showing through the crack. Whoever was in here, June guessed that was where they would be.

She took another deep breath, then shoved the door open as quickly and violently as possible so as to give herself an element of surprise. There was indeed a security guard inside watching a large bank of security monitors. He looked about how she had expected him to, if maybe a little younger and with a little less weight around the middle. He did have a half-eaten sandwich on the desk in front of him, and he was in the process of turning around in the chair when she barged him. Although he didn't say anything, his wide eyes clearly said that this was absolutely not a possibility he had considered occurring to him today.

The security guard slowly raised his hands. The look on his face suggested he didn't completely believe that the petite woman in front of him was really going to shoot him right in the head, but he didn't really want to test that theory.

"I don't know who you are or how you got here," he said, "but there's nothing good going to come from this."

"I've already seen that, with what you people did to Maury and the rest of his team," June said. "But I'm not going to go out that easily."

The guard furrowed his brow. "What are you talking about?"

"You know exactly what I'm talking about."

"No, I don't. How do you know Maury? Is he around here?"

June almost lowered her gun. This guy didn't seem to be in on the execution earlier, but there was no way of knowing for sure. She had assumed that everyone on the security team would be knowledgeable about what had happened, but perhaps that wasn't the case.

"He's dead," June said simply.

"Dead?" the security guard asked. "That can't be true. I just spoke to him a couple of hours ago when he was on the surface. He was going to get me…

uh, something I wanted from up there. I would have been told if something had happened to him since."

The guard seemed genuinely distraught at the idea that something had happened to Maury, but June still kept the gun up. "You're telling me you seriously don't have any idea what Logane ordered your security team to do earlier?"

"Lady, I don't have a security team. I'm just some grunt Logane has hired to keep an eye on the workers and make sure no one's stealing anything," he said, gesturing at the monitors. "The closest thing to a security team around here that's more than a glorified set of mall cops is Logane's private merc teams. If they did something, they sure as hell wouldn't have told me. They would never even give me so much as the time of day."

He could still be lying, June realized, but she would have to put the gun down eventually. She couldn't simply aim it at him all day. She relaxed her stance a little, but not enough that the guard would think she was just going to let this go. "I need the security footage from about half hour to an hour ago, all the areas around the submarine docks."

"Why would I give you…"

"I am still the one with the gun, and I think after you see that you'll realize that you're just as much in over your head in all this as I am."

"Lady, I've been in over my head since I got here," the guard said. He put his hands down. "Every single thing in this park is way bigger than it should be given my pay grade. And unfortunately I can't give you that footage."

"Just do it and…"

"No, I can't. Not that I won't, there just isn't any footage to give you. I was given an order from those mercs to shut down those cameras for the day. They said it came down directly from Logane, so I didn't want to question it. Whatever you're saying happened there, there's no record of it."

Crap. June had really hoped that would be the smoking gun she could bring with her back to the surface. But before she could get too upset over the fact, another thought occurred to her. "Did they tell you to shut down the cameras for anywhere else recently?"

"A whole bunch of them. That's probably why you were able to get in here without me seeing you. There's no telling what else anyone could be doing and I wouldn't be able to do my job. I swear, I better not get fired because you were able to get in here."

"That's… that's really your biggest concern right now? I just told you people are being killed by mercs, and you're concerned about your job?"

"You don't really think I would believe that, right?" From the way his voice cracked slightly, June could tell he actually might, but didn't want to admit it yet.

"Turn all the cameras back on that you were told to turn off. If they didn't want you to see anything in multiple places, there might still be something going on."

Slowly the guard did as he was told, keeping his eye on the gun the entire time. A number of the blank monitors came back on, revealing various places throughout the complex. June risked looking away from the guard long enough to see if there was anything happening on any of them. At first there was nothing, and June was afraid there wasn't going to be anything here she could use, and she had revealed herself to the guard for nothing. Then she caught something moving just out of the corner of one of the screens as someone left the frame.

"That one," June said. "That camera right there. Where is that? Are there any other cameras in the area?"

"That's the walkways over one of the tanks. I think it might be the one over…" The guard paused, realizing he was about to say something he probably wasn't supposed to reveal to random strangers, even if they were waving a gun.

"If you're trying to avoid saying what the attractions are here, you're a bit late with that revelation," June said. "I've already seen quite a few."

"It's weird, isn't it?" he said, almost reverently. "Seeing all these things in real life?"

"Do you know where they came from?" June asked. "Were they found or were they made?"

"That answer is way above my pay grade," the guard said again. She got the impression that was an excuse he got a lot of mileage out of around here. "Uh, that camera is in the area above the megalodon enclosure. There's a couple other cameras in the area. Let me toggle through their feeds and see if they show anything."

He hit a couple of buttons, and the video on the monitor changed to a different angle of that room. From this perspective, the megalodon tank looked like a vast swimming pool with many crisscrossing catwalks going over it. A glance at a few of the other monitors showed June that most of the areas over the exhibits must look like this. It suddenly occurred to her just how incredibly hard it would be to maintain a zoo of this sort. The amounts of food they would need to feed the creatures would be staggering. Did they harvest fish and sea life from around them in the ocean in order to do that, or did they have to ship in meat from elsewhere in the world and secretly bring it down in subs like the one she had come in on? The logistics of keeping a place like this not just up and running but also a secret must have been staggering.

Two of the mercs were standing at the edge of a platform overlooking the water, and for a moment they were the only people in the shot. Then a door opened along the wall and several people in jumpsuits like the one June was currently wearing stumbled through, their hands up over their heads and their faces showing obvious fear and confusion. Behind them there were three more armed guards, including the one that looked like he might be in charge of them, with Logane bringing up the rear. Logane actually appeared bored, like he could think of a large number of things more interesting he could be doing instead of going around the complex with his own personal death squad.

"What the hell?" the security guard muttered. June didn't say anything. She was pretty sure she was about to see these people shot again, just like earlier, and she didn't want to watch, but she knew she had to.

"Is there any sound on these cameras, or is it just video?" June asked.

"No sound," the guard said. "There's too much ambient noise for..."

He didn't finish the sentence, because that was the moment the mercs pushed the jumpsuited workers into the water.

The workers all had several seconds to thrash about, some trying to get back up on the platform, before the megalodon came up from underneath them. June suddenly found the lack of sound to be a blessing, because she didn't want to hear the screams as all these people were ripped apart by the monster from below. Logane and the mercs casually left the room, leaving the workers to die alone.

CHAPTER EIGHT

The two of them stood for over a minute in perfect silence, both of them staring at the churning cloud of bloody water that completely covered the screen now. As June started to come back to herself, she realized that she had unknowingly lowered her gun so it was pointing more at the security guard's knee now rather than his face. This would have been the perfect time for him to try to escape her or wrest the gun away, but he hadn't made any move of the sort. This man was just as in shock as she was, if not more so. June, after all, had already seen that Logane was capable of murder. She just hadn't understood yet how brutal and depraved he could truly be.

"This… this doesn't make any sense," the guard said. "Why would he do that?"

June still wasn't completely sure of the answer to that. If Logane truly intended for this place to be open to the public at some point, there was no reason for him to kill off so many people who just knew about the existence of Trenchland and its attractions. There was more here, and probably more even than Maury had been able to save to his thumb drive. She just didn't have any idea where to go to start deciphering what that might be.

She lowered the gun all the way. Hopefully, by this point, the guard was going to be more afraid of Logane than of her. "What's your name?" she asked.

"I… what? Why does it matter? I… what is…" He continued to stare at the screen. He didn't even seem to realize anymore that he wasn't being held by gunpoint.

"Tell me your name," she repeated, this time more forcefully. Finally he tore his gaze away from the screen and back to her.

"Mark. Mark Chush."

"Mark. I need you to think really hard about what you just saw. He just had those people killed. And he did it right where it was possible for you to see it, even if he did believe you would probably follow orders and have the camera off. So think for a second and tell me what that means about what he's going to do next."

"Wait, are you implying that he's going to have me killed as well?" Mark asked. "I haven't done anything that… that…" He trailed off as he looked at the monitors again. Logane and his personal army of mercs had left the area over the megalodon's enclosure. June caught a brief glimpse of them on one of the other monitors as they came down a hallway in an orderly fashion, possibly on their way to do something similar to someone else.

"Shit, you may be right," Mark said. "But… they wouldn't know that I just witnessed that, right? Caslaw told me to turn off the cameras, and there's no reason he would assume I disobeyed."

"Turning off the cameras results in no evidence of the crime, but that doesn't mean they're just going to assume you haven't figured something out."

"Oh crap," Mark mumbled to himself. "Oh shit. I am so dead."

"That's why you've got to help me, okay?" June said. "Help me find more evidence, and more importantly, help me get out of here so I can tell someone on the surface."

"Wait, I still don't even know who you are," Mark said. "And how the hell are you here?"

"My name's June Reilly. I'm a reporter. Maury snuck me in here because he knew there was a lot more going on down here than just a few creatures that aren't supposed to exist. But I don't think even he was prepared for it to be as bad as this."

"So, then, Maury's really dead? Just like those people we just saw."

"Not exactly like that, but yeah."

"Oh Christ. Oh crap. Oh shit."

Mark seemed very much in danger of trailing off into a muttering stupor. June couldn't have that. This guy was her only lifeline at the moment. "Mark. Stop. Please. Focus. Neither of us are going to get out of this if you break down completely."

"Right," Mark muttered, then, after a few seconds, he said it again with more conviction. "Right. I guess we can't stay here."

"Can you download and save that video we just saw before we go? Even with anything else I already have, that could be the smoking gun on everything."

"Uh, yeah," Mark said. He pulled a new thumb drive out of the drawer in a nearby desk and plugged it into the computer in front of him. As he went about downloading the video, June kept an eye on the monitors. She saw the mercs moving at a brisk pace on several different ones, going somewhere with urgency and intention.

"Are any of these cameras nearby this room?" June asked.

"Yeah. They are definitely getting closer. Just hold on a few more seconds… okay." He pressed a few more keys and then pulled the thumb drive out.

June held out her hand for it, and although Mark hesitated he did finally hand it over. "So, um, I hope you know where it is you want to go. I can probably take you wherever, but I'm not exactly used to having to run and hide from my coworkers."

"Wherever it is that we would need to go in order to get out of Trenchland," June said. She looked at the thumb drive in her hand, put it in her purse, and double checked to make sure that the other one was still there too. She kept the gun out, though, just in case. She didn't think she was going to need it anymore for Mark, but if they ran into Logane or his goons she doubted that was a situation that could be ended with just a friendly word. "Also, maybe there's somewhere we can go where I can check the contents of the other thumb drive I got from Maury's locker."

"I really don't think we have time for that, do you?" Mark asked.

"Not at the moment. And maybe it wouldn't be worth the time. But then again, there's also the possibility that something on there could point us in the direction of more information or evidence here in the theme park, and it would be a shame to only learn that once we were back on the surface."

Mark sighed but then nodded his head. "I don't know if I can promise you anything on that, but I do have a few ideas. Now's not the time to share them, though. The very first thing we have to do before anything else is not be in this room by the time anyone else gets here."

There was only the one door out of the main monitoring room, but in the outer security office there were two doors, one that led out into the public areas and another that went into the back halls where June had found herself earlier. Mark hesitated before picking a direction.

"It would be too easy for them to find us in the main thoroughfares," Mark said, "but the last camera I saw them on made it look like they were taking the back halls. So we'll have to go out the main way, I think."

"How do you know they wouldn't be sending people from both directions?" June asked.

"They could, I suppose, but that would imply that they think they need to sneak up on me because I know something. And if that's the case, I think we'd both simply be screwed."

June wasn't sure yet exactly how much she trusted this man to make decisions for them both, but she did know she didn't have any time to hesitate and think through every option. If Mark thought going out into the main parts of the park was the best option for the moment, then she figured she had to trust his judgement.

Back out in the main halls, they soon found themselves in front of a large tank that was darker than most. There weren't a lot of lights here, probably so visitors would better be able to see whatever was supposed to be in the exhibit. There were also some pallets of construction supplies for what looked like souvenir kiosks which they could duck down behind if anyone came in this general direction. It was as good a place as any for them to stop, catch their breaths, and come up with a better plan. Something glowed deep in the darkness of the tank, though, a pair of piercing blue eyes that seemed to follow them. They obviously wouldn't be in danger from whatever was in there, but June didn't want to stick around in this area with that thing watching them for any longer than she had to.

"Okay, so we're safe for the moment," June said to Mark. "Tell me you have a plan."

"Me? You're the one who broke in here and snooped. I would think plans would be your part of this," Mark said.

"I can't make plans unless I have more info, so spill," June said.

"Uh, right," Mark said. "So you want to escape and maybe check that drive you have, right?" He thought for a second and said, "Sure. Alright. The escape is the easy part. I get the impression that a lot of corners were cut when they built this place, but one thing they couldn't skimp on was a quick way out, if for no other reason than to make sure the richest man in the world wouldn't drown."

"Does he have his own personal escape pod or something?" June asked.

"Probably. And it's probably better than all the others. But there are public escape subs as well."

"So they're like life rafts on a ship or something?" she asked.

Mark shrugged. "Or something. The impression I got is that most of them aren't what you would call 'up to code,' although technically there isn't any such thing as a 'code' for a place like this. There was talk about accidents during building and filling this place, but no one ever really wanted to talk about it for fear of losing their jobs."

"Or their lives," June said. Mark looked uncomfortable with that but didn't disagree.

"So there's no government safety inspections or codes when it comes to this place. And it doesn't fall under any particular country's laws," he said. "Just as a heads up. You know, in case we get to one of the escape subs and it doesn't even work."

That was hardly something June wanted to hear, but they didn't have time to worry about that right now. They would approach that problem if and when they came to it.

"So where are these escape subs?" June asked.

"There's stations for them all the way around the perimeter of the complex," Mark said. "And a few on the roof area, but those are the ones for Logane and his people. They're more likely to be watched."

"How far away are we from the edge of the complex?"

"We're fairly close to the middle, so getting to the escape subs without being seen is going to take some work."

"Crap," June said. "What about the other thing? Some place where I would be able to check the thumb drive."

Mark had to take a moment to think about that before he answered. "Assuming Maury didn't put any fancy security measures or passwords on that drive, you could probably access it from any computer. But there aren't a lot of those in the public areas. There might be a few offices here and there with the right equipment, but the only ones that I know for certain would have the right computers would be the security stations."

"A lot of good that does us," June said. "Those mercs are probably crawling over your security office as we speak."

"The one we were just in, sure," Mark said. "But that's just the central security office. It's a large complex designed to have a lot of security when everything is said and done. So there's a few smaller stations that I might be able to lead you to along the way."

June nodded. "Okay. Sounds good. Let's get going then, Mark. I'm putting my life in your hands."

Mark looked less than enthusiastic about that, but he still led the way.

CHAPTER NINE

It was right about the time that June realized how lucky she had been in avoiding Logane's goons up until now that the luck started to run out. Using what little bit of spatial awareness of the place she had picked up so far, along with an assist from the sort-of-but-not-quite-accurate map, she got the impression that they were heading in the general direction of the far end of the complex from where she had entered at the sub docks. They were in an area with the signage "Monsters of the Eocene," but where most of the tanks seemed to not have anything in them. June was just trying to remember whether or not she knew what "the Eocene" was supposed to be when they heard voices approaching them from ahead.

"Crap," Mark said as he heard them. "We need to go back." Except before they could even turn around, they started to hear shouts from that direction as well.

"Please tell me you know some other way around here," June said.

"No, I don't… wait. Maybe I do. I don't think you'll like it though."

"At this point, whether or not I like it isn't going to factor much into my decisions. Just lead the way."

He took her hand and pulled her to an innocuous door nearby that, like so many others, opened for them easily when it probably shouldn't have. There were more halls here, but most notably there was a metal staircase leading both up and down. Mark paused at the downward stairs for a moment like he were considering something, then instead led June upward. June didn't question him, instead just following him up approximately four stories of stairs. June had thought she was in pretty good shape, but by the time they made it to where they were going she was out of breath. Mark seemed even worse off. June supposed he hadn't really had a need to keep toned when all he had to do most days was watch over a mostly-empty complex. There were still more stairs heading up, but at this level there was a landing and another door, which he led her through. After they were down another hall and through another entryway, they were finally at where June assumed he had been leading her the entire time.

She recognized the place they were as being very similar to the room they had seen on the security monitors where Logane's people had fed the workers to the megalodon, although this room wasn't nearly as huge as that one. They were above the water tank with a couple of walkways going over it, but whatever was supposed to be in this particular water must have been much smaller than the megalodon.

"Alright, so where do we go from here?" she asked.

"There's a tunnel we can go through," Mark said. "It's not something most people would think about using, so it's our best bet to avoid Caslaw and the rest of the mercs."

June looked around, but she didn't see anything along the walls of the room that looked like it might be the entrance of a tunnel. "Where is it?"

Mark gave a bemused look. "It's through there," he said, pointing down at the water.

June paused long enough to give him the chance to say that he was joking, but he never said anything of the sort. "You have got to be out of your goddamned mind," June said. "There is absolutely nowhere in this place that I would dare swim through to get anywhere. Especially since there's no way anyone would design an escape hatch that could only be accessed by nearly drowning yourself first."

"No, that's not… look. This isn't intended as an escape hatch or secret tunnel or something. It's a maintenance tunnel. They run throughout the complex, and there's no security cameras in them, at least not yet. We can use it to get to one of the emergency escape subs that are around the complex."

June looked down into the pool of water, expecting something to jump out of it and get her. When the water remained still, she looked back at Mark. "There isn't any other way to get into the tunnels?"

"There's lots of other ways in and out of the tunnels. And right now, all of them would require us to go someplace currently crawling with Logane's mercs."

"But what's supposed to be in this tank?" June asked. "They wouldn't just make a random tank and put it here."

"There shouldn't be anything in it yet."

"What do you mean yet?"

"I mean that whatever they were developing to put in here, no security reports about it have crossed my desk. I got a report any time some new creature was added."

"Are you sure that someone wasn't just too busy being, I don't know, dead from Logane's goons and couldn't take time out of gasping their last breath to get you the report?"

Mark paused, suddenly looking worried. "I... I don't think that would be the case. I know that the creature that was supposed to be in this tank was called *Enchodus Petrosus*. I looked it up once and apparently it was supposed to be some kind of prehistoric herring? So even if it is in here, it's not something we're going to need to worry about, okay?"

June took a deep breath. After everything she had seen so far tonight, especially the most recent events in the megalodon tank, she had a sneaking suspicion that she was well on her way to developing a deep phobia of going into any body of water bigger than a bathtub. But whether she had a building terror or not, her survival instinct was enough that she would do anything to stay alive, and right now there was a much deeper danger from the mercs than from whatever may or may not be in there. And Mark was right. If something was in there, it was likely harmless from his description.

"I can't go in there..." she started to say.

"Look, I don't think we have time to..."

"Let me finish. I was going to say I can't go in there without finding some way to waterproof this."

She held up her purse for him to see. "It's got my phone and both of the thumb drives. If they get wet we'll lose every piece of evidence I have about Logane and Trenchland."

"Oh," Mark said, then started looking around. "There should be some crates or coolers around here where they keep meat to feed the animals. I think they usually wrap the food in plastic. Maybe there's something like that around that we can use to keep them dry."

That didn't exactly sound like the best plan to June, but for now it was the only plan they had. On the main platform off to the side they found a pallet full of boxes, one of which was open and half full of dried, vacuum-sealed meat or jerky of some kind. If they opened the packages carefully, there would probably be enough to wrap around the individual electronics, as well as June's gun, and then wrap her whole purse in it just to be on the safe side. Mark immediately got to it removing the meat, but June paused and considered the box. Why would half the meat in the box already be gone?

"Mark, are you sure they haven't gotten around to putting the fish in this tank yet?" she asked.

"Reasonably sure," Mark said. "Why do you ask?"

It's probably nothing, June thought. *Somebody probably just came over from one of the other enclosures to get meat for one of the other exhibits.*

"Uh, just forget it," June said. "Besides, as you said, it's just herring anyway."

Why would anybody be feeding chunks of freeze-dried meat to herring? she wondered, then forced the thought out of her mind.

Once she had plastic wrapped around her gun, the thumb drives, and cell phone, she wrapped the outside of her purse the best she could given the quality of the materials they had. She would still be able to keep the strap around her head and shoulder so her hands would be completely free while she swam, but the main part of the bag was covered.

They both stood at the edge of the water, but neither of them was eager to be the first to jump in. "So once we're in, where exactly in there are we trying to go?"

"If we jump in from that catwalk over there, we'll be able to swim up against that wall," he said, indicating a specific place along a far wall. "Underneath the wall right where I'm pointing there's an overhang with a hatch. I should be able to get there first and open it. Luckily the keycodes for the hatches to the maintenance tunnels haven't been set up yet, like most of them around this place."

"Why the hell would you need a key code to get through the hatch from the water?" June asked. "Do you have a big problem with fish trying to break in where they don't belong?"

"You may think you're joking, but that's actually kind of correct. Most of the creatures here, no one knew what they were or weren't capable of before they showed up here. Most of them are the big dumb carnivorous fish you would expect them to be, but just last week the shastasaurus figured out how to open up the maintenance hatch in its own tank. People would be afraid of it escaping if it weren't the size of a goddamned whale. Since then we haven't wanted to take any chances that the smaller creatures might be just as smart."

June looked at him to see if he was kidding, but there was nothing on his face that made her think he was telling anything but the truth. "So we have to worry about the exhibits escaping and coming after us in the tunnels?"

"No, we don't," Mark said. "Not in the tunnels. But if these things ever got out and loose in the open sea? There's no telling what they could do."

They both moved to the area on the catwalks closest to the place on the wall they were aiming for. "Now, uh, I think we need to move quickly," Mark said. "Not just to hold our breaths, but because the water is much colder than you would expect. Without any wetsuits, it could probably really screw with us if we take too long. Got it?"

"Got it," June said. "Um, are you going to go first?"

Mark took a deep breath. "I guess I have to," he said, then with no further preamble he climbed over the catwalk railing and jumped in. June gave him just long enough to swim out of the way so she wouldn't land on him, and then she did the same.

Even knowing how cold the water would be, it was still an intense shock to her system. It took all of her willpower not to accidentally suck in a lungful of the water when the temperature hit her. She immediately came back up to the surface for a gasp of air and looked around to see if Mark had done the same. All she could see was a vague silhouette in the water as he swam directly for the approximate location of the hatch. June herself swam closer to the wall before she too submerged.

This particular tank wasn't as dark as some of the ones she had seen. There was a diffuse light coming from some source below them, enough that she could see Mark ahead of her and see the underwater overhang that would be where they would find the maintenance tunnel.

Out of the corner of her eye, she caught a flicker of shadow.

She whipped her head around to where she thought it had been, but there didn't seem to be anything there. Yet when she turned her head back, there was another flicker, this time below her. She looked down. This time she was positive that something swam just out of her view at the last second.

They were not alone in this tank.

Ahead of her, Mark was right at the overhang and fiddling with a circular handle. It didn't seem to be budging as he tried to turn it, but he didn't look overly worried yet. June paused, torn between going to him and instead going back to the surface. She had almost decided to turn back around when Mark's movements got a little jerkier. Instinct kicked in, and she swam up next to him to add her own strength to turning the hand.

It budged and turned just as something flashed up from beneath and grabbed Mark by the leg. His mouth opened and a cloud of bubbles came out as he was pulled lower. June reached out and grabbed his hand, at which point she was able to look down and get a better idea of what had attacked him. A huge fish, about as long as she was tall, had latched onto his calf and was frantically thrashing in an attempt to pull him down. It wouldn't have looked like anything terrifying or prehistoric if it weren't for the huge tusk-like teeth protruding from the front of its upper and lower jaws. As blood clouded around the struggling pair and Mark sank deeper, pulling June with her, she saw five or six more of the killer fish swimming up from the depths and heading right for them.

June only had a split second to make the decision. She knew immediately it was one she was going to question for the rest of her life, however long that might be. She let his hand slip through her fingers and thrust herself with all her might upward to the door, catching the handle and turning it the rest of the way and causing the hatch to swing open toward her. She could vaguely hear muffled screams echoing through the water as more of the fish came up and grabbed Mark, but June knew she didn't have any time to look down and give him one final glance. He was a goner, and so would she be if she hesitated.

June pulled herself up through the open door and into the cramped maintenance tunnel just as something sharp scraped at the heels of her shoes. She yanked her legs out of the water and saw fangs flashing just below the surface. They disappeared, along with any other sign of the fish, as the water turned a deep red.

Right next to the hatch there was a small etched plaque, apparently there so whoever was going through the maintenance tunnels would be able to identify which tank they were at.

Enchodus Petrosus, the plaque said, and then, right under that, A.K.A. *The Sabretooth Herring.*

CHAPTER TEN

For perhaps the first time in June Reilly's life, she felt like giving up. She hadn't felt any particular affinity for Mark Chush, but with him gone she was again alone in a facility deep beneath the surface of the ocean, possibly being pursued by someone who had proven himself capable of murder and surrounded by monsters out of history and legend who were fully capable of carrying that man's wishes out for him.

She lay there in the semi-dark of the maintenance tunnel, and for a time she didn't move. Slowly, though, her typical resolve returned to her. She wasn't going to let herself die. She still had work to do, exposing Dom Logane's nefarious deeds to the rest of the world. As she came to her senses she started to pay more attention to her surroundings. The maintenance tunnel was small enough that she would have to go through it on her hands and knees, but beyond the space where she was currently lying it was completely dry. There were small lights at long intervals along the tunnel, enough for her to see by but still little enough light to cause long deep shadows in all the corners where anything could be lurking. That thought almost made her afraid, but she had to remind herself that all of the terrors she had so far witnessed were in the water, not in the dry parts. It was unlikely, after all, that Logane would have brought back some kind of small carnivorous dinosaur when everything else had been of the sea.

Of course, she realized as she started what she was sure would be a long crawl to the emergency subs Mark had mentioned, it might not be right to say that Logane had "brought back" all these sea monsters like this was Jurassic Park. Some of them he could have found out in the world. But, given the mythical nature of some of their names that she had seen so far, it seemed more likely that everything here had been cooked up in some genetics lab. With that kind of technology, Logane could be curing diseases or ending world hunger, if he could just create any creature he wanted. Instead he was using it to create megalodons and Fiji Mermaids. June shook her head at the thought. Wealth was really wasted on the rich.

It suddenly occurred to June that, in her rush to escape the killer fish and get as far from them as possible, she hadn't yet bothered to check on the state of her purse and all the precious evidence she had wrapped up inside. She felt a moment of panic as she unwrapped the plastic around the outside of her purse. The tape seal on the outer plastic wasn't nearly as tight as she had hoped, and despair began to overwhelm her as she realized that water had leaked in. Certain that all she was going to find was a bunch of unusable water-logged electronics, she opened the purse and took out each of the individually wrapped items. While the prognosis wasn't great, it was at least far better than she had thought it would be at first. Out of the four items she had put in the plastic bags, two had been soaked through. One of those was the gun. June took it out and inspected it, but she only had the most basic knowledge and training when it came to hand guns. She had no idea if the water would keep it from working if she needed to fire it before this was all over, and she certainly couldn't try to test fire it in this tunnel. She also had no idea if somehow salt water would be more damaging to a pistol or if the type of water didn't matter. She was going to be stuck with the luck of the draw if it came down to that.

The other bag that had leaked through was the second thumb drive, the one on which Mark had saved the video of the people being fed to the megalodon. The other two bags, containing her phone and Maury's thumb drive, had been wrapped tight enough that there didn't seem to be any damage, at least none that was visible to the naked eye. The loss of the second thumb drive was upsetting, but between the two of them, she believed that one was probably less important. Or, at least, she hoped it was. She still hadn't had a chance to actually look at Maury's drive and assess the quality of the evidence he had gathered.

As she tucked the items back into her purse (not bothering to wrap the gun again, but doing her best to wrap the second thumb drive just in case there was still a way to retrieve the data off of it), she thought again about whether or not it was important to view the contents of Maury's drive before she escaped, if escape was even possible at this point. Would she really gain anything by going out of her way looking for more clues and evidence? Surely she had to have enough to write the exposé of the century and air all of Logane's stinky laundry out for the world to smell.

Except there was something very basic about this whole situation that she kept coming back to, something that she couldn't get out of her head. If this place was eventually going to be open to the public, why kill the staff now? This had to be more than Logane trying to cover up a few accidental deaths or something during the construction of Trenchland.

She knew there had to be more to the story, and if she was going to have any clue whatsoever what else she might need to look for before she left here, then she needed to get an idea of what was on that drive.

Mark had given her some general directions on where to go to find the escape subs and another security station, but just to be sure she was headed in the right direction she pulled out the cartoonish map and tried to consult it. The map was a runny, waterlogged mess, but after she spent some time deciphering it and comparing it to things she heard Mark saying while they'd escaped, she thought she might have a general idea where she was going. In fact, while these maintenance tunnels seemed to primarily be for pipes and wiring, she thought it might actually take her right to one of the stations, assuming she didn't get lost along the way. So she kept crawling, trying to keep her eye on the prize the entire time.

Once or twice she did get turned around in the tunnels, but after passing several other hatches similar to the one she had initially come through, the tunnel widened and grew in height until she was able to stand and see a few more standard doors. Like the hatches, these had plates on them announcing where they went. It was funny how that worked. The signage back here was up while none was up in the more standard halls. She supposed the tunnels had a higher chance of making someone lost, and someone had taken the initiative needed to make sure that didn't happen.

Still, even when she found a sign announcing she was at "Security Station D," she hesitated before opening it. With her luck so far, the door could be mislabeled and she was about to walk right in on where the mercs hung out in their off time. She placed her ear to the door and, when she didn't hear anything other than an electronic humming from the other side, she slowly opened it. The room beyond was similar to the security office where she had found Mark, but it was smaller and didn't appear to have a separate room with security monitors. There was just a desk with a computer on it and something that looked like a small holding cell for any unruly guests. June checked to make sure the computer was working, then pulled out the thumb drive from Maury and plugged it in.

Any worries June had that this drive wouldn't work anymore disappeared right away. There were hundreds, maybe even a thousand, files saved to the drive. They were divided up into various folders, often with non-explanatory or esoteric names like

"Cretaceous 75-B" and "That invoice from the printer incident."

June paused as she stared at the screen full of information, finding herself both excited and disappointed at the same time. Excited because, with everything here, there was no way she wouldn't have plenty to go on to nail Logane to the wall. Disappointed, though, because there was no way she could browse through all this quickly and get any idea of further info she might need before she escaped. At random she picked a folder, then a subfolder within it, and read a random file. It was a copy of an email chain, but as she skimmed it she realized the people on either side of the conversation were intentionally being vague on what they were saying. Based on the last email, which said simply "Tell J that the price is acceptable for BW 32, but will need to continue negotiating on BW 106," she assumed there was some kind of business transaction going on. Once she combed through the rest of the data she might be able to figure out what they were talking about, but that wasn't going to happen now.

So deep was her disappointment that she almost ejected the thumb drive without looking any further, but at the last second she realized she had missed the name of the very first file in the very first folder.

She stared at it for a second, just to make sure she was reading it right:

JUNE REILLY OPEN THIS FIRST

Maury had specifically left a message with her name on it. That was dangerous if this thumb drive had ended up in someone else's hands before he'd been able to get it to her, and Maury likely would have realized that, so it had to be important if he was willing to take a chance and record her name so blatantly on the drive. June took a deep breath to prepare herself for whatever she might see, then clicked on the file.

A video screen popped up, with Maury front on center. He seemed to be in a room very similar to this one, maybe even on this very same computer for all June knew. From his clothing and the state of his beard hair, June suspected he had recorded this right before he had come to the surface to get her.

"June, if you're seeing this, then they offed me. I didn't want to believe that was going to happen, and hopefully it didn't leave you alone trying to find your way through Trenchland. If I'm able to present this to you personally and help you back to the surface, I will likely tell you to ignore this file. So maybe you disobeyed that instruction and watched this anyway out of curiosity. If that's the case, you likely won't need to know anything I have to say here. If that isn't the case, and you manage to see this before you even leave the complex, then there's one more thing you have to do before you leave the complex."

June leaned forward toward the screen and listened intently.

"You have to destroy Trenchland. You have to make sure that nothing here ever makes it to see the light of the surface."

CHAPTER ELEVEN

June watched the rest of the video with an odd mix of shock and horror and wonder, and when it finished she started it again from the beginning, even though she knew she didn't have time for this. She just needed to make sure she didn't misunderstand a single thing Maury said.

"By now you'll have seen some of the stuff that's in here," Maury said as the second viewing continued. "I don't know exactly which exhibits you'll have seen and not seen, but if you're as smart as I think you are, you'll have wondered where they came from. And I'm telling you, based on what I have on this drive, I don't think Logane just found weird monsters throughout the world and brought them here. I think they were made, from the smallest prehistoric jellyfish to whatever that disquieting tentacled thing is at the bottom of that pit. And they sure as hell weren't made to show off to tourists. There's too much evidence on this drive to suggest that any attempt to prepare Trenchland for tourists was just to throw off the people building it. As for what exactly these creatures are for if not that, well, I have a few guesses, but I'm not the reporter here. I'm betting you will be able to put the data I have into a better picture than I could.

"But whatever that picture ends up being, it's bad. Really bad. I hope you've seen enough by now to realize that and believe me. This place needs to be wiped out. If you're watching this before you escape from Trenchland, then you still have a chance to do exactly that. I've done what I can to set it all up for you. You just need to knock it all down, both figuratively and literally."

At this point, Maury's speech went into an amount of technical engineering jargon that June didn't completely understand, but the important points were obvious enough. Maury's role had been important enough here that he'd been able to make a few subtle engineering adjustments, the kind that would make it easier to destroy the whole place with just a couple of well-placed explosives. The explosives should be near where they needed to go off. All June had to do was detonate them and then get to the nearby escape sub.

As the video came to an end again, June considered watching it a third time. But she didn't think her understanding of the situation would change any. She understood as much as she needed to, and she had all the directions and instructions she needed to make it happen.

With the thumb drive back in her purse, June quietly went back through the door she had come through. There had been no indication that Logane's people had been approaching her position, but she felt like she was very close to having this hell night finally be over, and the last thing she wanted was to get a bullet between her eyes right as she was about to cross the finish line. The directions Maury had given in the video led her in roughly the direction she had intended to go anyway, as far as Mark's instructions on reaching an escape pod. She was just going to have to make a small detour first.

Having the signs on the doors in the maintenance tunnel was a big help in keeping her from getting lost again, and she soon found one with a sign marked "Moses." According to Maury this was the room where he had set everything up, but there had been no indication in the video, nor was there any on the door, as to who or what Moses was supposed to be. It shouldn't matter, of course, since whatever creature was housed beyond was going to be in a tank, and the spot Maury had indicated would be in the actual room.

Most of the rooms and halls she had passed through up to this point had been in various states of being unfinished, but this was the most incomplete one she had come across so far. There were exposed girders throughout the room and places where walls were obviously supposed to go at some point. There was no way of telling what was planned for here beyond the giant window on one side of the room showing onto yet another huge tank of water. There were pallets with building supplies all over, giving many places where one could hide in the spacious room. On the far side there was an archway leading back into the main halls. According to everything she had heard from both Maury and Mark, she should be able to find one of the emergency escape sub stations not far beyond that door. But this room specifically was the one where Maury had set up his ludicrous plan to send the entire complex to the bottom of the trench.

According to Maury, there was a specific set of floor to ceiling girders that needed to be blown up. This would cause a domino effect of collapsing structural supports that would bring the entire place down within fifteen to twenty minutes. It sounded implausible to June, but she wasn't the one who had knowledge of these things. If he said it was going to work, then she would just have to trust that he had spent a lot of time figuring this out and making certain it would work.

Except, as she found the spot where she was supposed to put the explosives, a very big problem began to present itself. Maury had said the explosives would be here, and he had given her instructions on how to set them up. But there were no explosives. She wondered just how or why exactly explosives would be in this area. Maybe they were left over from mining out pieces of the rock in the side of the trench that Trenchland hung over. Or maybe Maury had smuggled them in. Whatever the reason, these explosives didn't seem to exist now. She looked all around at the various pallets, thinking that they would have to have been hidden somewhere. The only clue she could find as to their potential whereabouts was a square space on the floor where the dust wasn't as thick, as though there had been a pallet there that had been moved elsewhere. If that was where Maury had hidden them, then they were long gone to some other distant part of the complex, and June's plans to destroy this place were pretty much screwed.

June stared at the place where the steel girders met the floor and couldn't help but think of the movie *Star Wars*. The Rebels in that one had destroyed the Death Star with a carefully placed explosive that caused an improbable chain reaction, something that had always not sat well with her as a movie goer. It had just felt too easy. Yet now here she was with a very similar situation in front of her. A part of her was almost annoyed that the scenario she had felt was so unlikely in fiction was now going to be exactly what she needed to set in motion in the real world.

But a much bigger part of her didn't care. She just wanted this whole terrible place to sink to the bottom of the ocean, and she suddenly felt completely determined not to leave until that had happened.

There was, of course, the problem of how she was even going to make this part collapse without any dynamite or anything.

"Come on, Maury," June muttered to herself. "What were you planning to do as a backup? If this really was your plan, then there had to be some other way to make it happen if something went wrong."

Something moved deep in the darkness of the tank next to her, and June paused, terrified and yet somehow completely fascinated at the idea of what might be inside. There were no lights anywhere in the tank to illuminate it, but after some time she thought she saw something slither through the water, something huge and slightly serpentine with four massive flippers to propel it through the water.

Wait, I think I know this one, she thought. *A mosasaurus*? That might explain where the name Moses came from. Another flash through the water revealed an almost crocodilian head. She wasn't completely confident that her guess was correct, but she figured she had to be in the right ballpark. There hadn't been any other signage added to this area yet that could confirm or deny her suspicions. It was undeniably huge, however, and June found herself wondering how much danger she would be in if that thing suddenly decided she looked tasty and rammed the glass to get her. The glass would have to be incredibly thick to hold back the pressure of the deep-sea waters, or at least that would be the way someone with any sense would design it. From Maury's video and his talk about what it would take to bring this whole thing down, she suspected it was possible that the thickness of the glass could be another place where costs had been cut with no care about safety.

She looked at the mosasaurus again, then back at the girder that was supposed to be a weak point. Even if it was weaker than the rest of the structural supports around it, which still just seemed so improbable to June, what would possibly need to happen to it to take it out?

Could something ramming into it at high speeds possibly do the trick?

Okay, she thought to herself. *The plan forming in my head doesn't exactly seem like the most logical thing. But so little about what I've seen here fits typical common-sense logic. So just maybe what if?*

She was just starting to contemplate how she might accomplish this when she heard sounds coming through the main archway. There were the sounds of a number of footsteps, along with two men talking and shouting orders at the others.

It looked like, after keeping ahead of them all night, June's time was finally up. Logane and his mercenaries had finally found her.

CHAPTER TWELVE

June had just enough warning that she could hide in one of the darker corners behind a stack of unused building supplies. She kept her line of sight on the main door, though, so she saw as Logane and his death squad came in.

Dom Logane did not look anywhere near as dapper or handsome as he had earlier when June had first seen him. The hours in between must have really put the stress on him, since his formerly practiced movements were now tired and jerky, and there seemed to be a growing, uncontrollable tic of rage at the edge of his mouth.

The most notable difference of all, though, was that his pristine clothes now had many different spatters of blood on them, more than would have just been left behind by murdering Maury and his group. There wouldn't have been any on him from the people who'd been killed in the water by the

Megalodon, so he and his goon squad must have been busy in the meantime. June wondered if there even were any innocent workers or contractors left in the whole complex, or if June, Logane, and his hired mercs were all that was left.

For the moment, neither Logane nor any of his current armed bodyguards seemed to be able to see her peering out from behind the pillars in the dark. "Whoever you are, show yourself and I promise you won't be hurt," he called out. June wanted to call back and ask if he really thought she didn't know what he had been up to all night, but she decided that being quiet was the better option right now. If there was anything villains in stories hated, it was silence whenever the hero was around, and they always had to fill that silence with details on their plans, like they desperately wanted the hero to finally understand that the villain was just misunderstood. If June was lucky, Logane would fall into that pattern. On a whim, June very slowly reached into her purse and pulled out the phone. There wasn't a lot of charge left on it, but there would be enough for at least one more recording. She turned on the recording app and waited.

"I know you're not one of my workers," Logane called. June pulled herself deeper into the shadows of a corner, putting Logane and his people out of her eyesight, but the echoes in the half-finished room made it easy to hear his words even all the way over here. "We've already accounted for all of them. We caught a glimpse of you on one of the cameras earlier while you were with that security guard. You may be wearing coveralls of someone from here, but you don't have the right build, I would think. So what are you? Some kind of spy from some rival company? Was this supposed to be some kind of corporate espionage thing? If so, boy did you ever pick the wrong night to try it."

There was a random single gunshot, and June jumped, almost revealing her location, but the shot had gone off on the other side of the room. Logane, if he was actually the one firing and not one of his hired thugs, was just shooting at random trying to get her to reveal herself.

June glanced at the tank window to see the mosasaurus swimming closer, looking agitated. She had no idea what a gunshot from in here would sound like inside the massive water tank, but whatever it sounded like, it wasn't a sound the creature appreciated.

That might be it, June thought. *That might be my way to do this*.

"Unless that's not what you are at all," Logane said. "Wait. That's got to be it. One of them sent you, didn't they? Didn't they? Answer me!"

June knew it was just a ploy to get her to speak in the hopes that she would reveal her location, but she also felt like he was on the verge of finally spilling that key piece of evidence she wanted. Before she could rethink what a bad idea this was, she yelled out an answer.

"My boss says you have a lot of explaining to do," she said, then quickly ducked down and moved among the shadows to another pile of unused building materials. A shot rang out again, this time much closer to where she had just been, but still not close enough that she would have been in danger.

In the water, the mosasaur began to thrash about and moved closer to the glass.

"Your boss, huh? I suppose that probably makes you one of Jafarov's people. Am I right?"

June knew that name, although it took her a moment to place it. The most notable person with the surname Jafarov who had been in the news lately was a petty warlord/terrorist in Eastern Europe who had been linked to a handful of attacks. She thought again about things she had seen on the thumb drive, and finally it clicked.

This wasn't really ever intended to be an amusement park at all. That had all been for show, something to keep the people working on it under the impression that the ultimate goal was something benign.

But Trenchland wasn't a tourist attraction. It was both storage and showroom for biological weapons. That was what "BW" had meant in the email she'd seen.

"He's not happy with you," June yelled out, "and he's definitely not going to be happy that you're trying to kill me."

"Oh please. Jafarov is small fish compared to some of the others I've been talking to," Logane said. There was no gunshot accompanying his voice this time, which June suspected wasn't a good sign. She ducked down a little lower and reached into her purse. Her pistol was right there on top, but she wasn't sure how much that would help her. Even if the bullets didn't misfire from the water earlier, she only had the six shots, compared to whatever handgun Logane was carrying, along with the heavy-duty rifles being toted around by the mercs. In the silence she could hear the faint sound of clothing and boots as the mercs moved about. They were probably systematically searching the room while Logane distracted her, she realized.

"Some of the organizations, some of the world leaders that have come to me looking for a little something surprising that they can use against their enemies, you would be shocked to hear the names," Logane said. "And that's just for here. That's not even including the other facilities."

That line shocked her so much that she couldn't stop herself from saying something back. "What do you mean, other facilities?"

"You know exactly what other facilities I mean," Logane said. "Jafarov himself is the one who suggested we genetically engineer some..." He paused, and when he spoke again he was clearly furious. "You're not with Jafarov."

Even without seeing any of them, June knew one or more of the mercs had to be close. The instant they saw her, she knew they would gun her down. Given everything she had seen tonight, there was no way they would try to take her alive. So if she was going to try something, this was her last chance to do it.

From her current vantage point, she could just see the tank window right in front of the compromised girders. The mosasaurus was no longer within sight, but she was sure it was somewhere just beyond, and still agitated from the gunfire.

She pointed her gun at that spot on the glass, pulled back the hammer, and fired.

She apparently hadn't needed to worry about the water damaging it. The gun worked perfectly fine.

The bullet hit the glass, but it didn't shatter. The glass was thick enough, it seemed, that the bullet only took a small chunk out of it. But the mercs must have thought that was the general direction she had shot from, because they all turned their weapons and fired.

"No, you idiots!" Logane screamed. "Don't shoot at the glass!"

June took that moment of confusion to race for the archway. Bullets pinged and ricocheted off the glass, but none of them were enough to completely break it. June could hear it cracking, however, and she knew she didn't have a lot of time to get out of the room before the integrity of the glass finally failed.

She was right at the door to the main halls as Logane and the others realized where she actually was. They turned, getting ready to finally execute her, when the mosasaurus rammed into the window at full speed.

CHAPTER THIRTEEN

She knew full well that if she turned around to look at the spectacle, she would die, so she just kept running right under the archway as the room behind her filled with the sounds of shattering glass and the horrific roar of water spewing in. She felt numerous shards of something hit her painfully in the back, causing her to stumble, but she managed to keep standing long enough to get out the door before the flood of water knocked her off her feet and sent her sprawling. The water flowed over her and choked in her throat, and for several seconds she thought this would be the way she died, drowning in the water from the mosasaurus enclosure.

Quickly, though, she realized that even though the water was rushing over and around her, she wasn't fully submerged. It wasn't even that deep around her yet. She came to her senses long enough to look back into the room and see a quite unexpected sight. The head of the mosasaurus was all the way through the glass, but it was stuck. The rushing water was coming in from around its head as it thrashed and tried to get free. The creature was in fact the very thing keeping the whole area from flooding immediately.

The head was long enough, however, that it had hit the girder Maury had indicated and severely bent it. Metal was screaming in strain above and below it as the load-bearing beam could no longer hold what it was supposed to.

She could hear Logane and the mercs somewhere beyond all that chaos in the room, but the mosasaurus and the spurting wall of water cut them off from her. That didn't stop them from trying to shoot, but nothing was coming even close to her.

All of the confusion was going to buy her some time. She had to find that escape sub and get out of here before the events of this room caused a cascading effect that would soon bring down the entire complex.

From Maury's descriptions, the nearest escape sub-station should have been right out the door she had just come through, then down a long hall to a room in the shape of a half-circle where there would be several doors leading into a number of the subs. Just like everything else in Trenchland there was supposed to be clearly posted signage directing people where to go and what to do in an event just like this, but either the signs hadn't been installed yet or Logane had never truly intended to need them, at least not for civilians. June bet that kind of thing was most certainly present in his own personal area that led to his sub, of course.

Thankfully the room in question was fairly easy to find with Maury's instructions. Five water-tight doors were spread around the half-circle, each with a round handle similar to the one they'd found on the maintenance tunnel hatch. She hesitated for a moment, wondering if all the subs were operational or if any of them hadn't been properly installed yet or something. That moment of hesitation ended as she heard a renewed roar behind her, possibly from the mosasaurus but more likely from the water as the glass continued cracking and letting more of the tank's contents in. The floor in this room had been dry when she had entered it, but the carpet was rapidly getting soaked. For now the mosasaurus tank was probably the only one that was ruptured, but as the supports in the building failed she suspected other tanks would break open, and once that started it would probably progress very quickly. She wasn't going to have the time to inspect the subs to see which one was the most sea-worthy, not that she would really know what to look for anyway.

Also, while it was hard to tell with all the other noise, she thought she heard shouting from some of the mercs, maybe even more gunfire. Maybe they were trying to shoot the mosasaurus as it thrashed about and made things worse, or maybe they thought they were aiming at her. Either way, they could still come in here after her at any second. So June selected one of the doors at random, twisted the wheel handle, went in, and slammed the door behind her.

The interior of the escape sub was about the size of the inside of an SUV. There were a number of seats with buckles along the walls on either side, with two seats up front next to a control panel and a window. She sat in the seat and looked around for an on-switch of some kind. There was a big obvious switch in green, so she flipped that one and hoped for the best. Light came on in the interior and the control board lit up.

June looked down at the blinking controls and keys in front of her, but none of them made any sense at all as far as she could tell. This thing was designed to be something of a life raft, she assumed, so it would stand to reason that it was designed so that anyone would be able to use it and not just someone with special training. However, nothing about Trenchland so far had made her confidant that it was built with any kind of safety or OSHA standards in mind. Given it came from the mind of Dom Logane, a man who thought he was at the cutting edge of technology and design, maybe it would be better to assume it was severely over-designed.

"Sub? Can you hear me?" she asked. She wasn't really expecting it to respond, and yet somehow at the same time she wasn't at all surprised when it did.

"Thank you for using the Minerva Emergency-escape Submersible System. Before I can assist you, I need to adapt myself to your personal voice. Please say the following phrases after me."

"Oh for fuck's sake, you've got to be kidding me," June said.

"I am sorry, that is not one of the phrases I need you to say. Please say the following phrases after me."

June held back another swear word for fear that it would confuse the completely-superfluous digital assistant again. "Okay, fine. What are the phrases?"

"I am sorry, that is not one of the phrases I need you to say. Please say the following phrases after me. Would you like to go to the fair?"

"Would you like to go to the fair?" June replied, trying very hard, and probably not quite succeeding, at keeping her voice calm and measured.

"Zachary does not belong among us."

There were five more mostly nonsensical phrases, and June dutifully repeated each one. Finally Minerva seemed to reach the end. "Very good. We are now ready to begin any emergency escape procedures you may need. Please state where you would like this submersible to go."

"Just anywhere that's not here."

"I'm sorry, that is not a sufficient answer. Please state where you would like to go."

"Get me to the surface of the ocean. Is that sufficient enough for you?"

"Processing. Thank you. Beginning preparations to bring this submersible to the surface. Please buckle in, and thank you for using M.E.S.S."

June almost laughed despite herself before she remembered that this was the system that was supposed to get her somewhere safe. Instead, all that came out of her mouth was a restrained, tired croak.

Outside of the sub, she could hear the sound of metal bending, of things crashing, of water rushing in to fill the empty spaces inside Trenchland. The main window of the escape sub, however, faced front, ensuring that the only view she currently had was of a long tube that ended in some kind of hatch. The sub, she realized, was essentially going to be shot out of the tube like a bullet. A screen on the control panel displayed the number fifteen, then fourteen.

"For your safety, please buckle up," Minerva said. "We will not be able to launch until all passengers have done so."

June didn't have to be told that one twice. She immediately located the seatbelt on the chair she was in and firmly fastened herself in.

"All passengers must be buckled before we can continue," Minerva said as the countdown hit ten. "Failure to do so will result in a delay of the emergency launch."

"I'm buckled already," June yelled at the computer.

"Not all passengers are buckled," the computer said. The number on the screen hit five, then four. "Failure of all passengers to buckle will delay the launch."

"I said I'm buckled!" June screamed. "There's no one else here!" She looked around just to make sure she wasn't missing something. There was definitely no one else in the small escape sub.

"Not all passengers are buckled," Minerva said cheerfully. "Emergency launch has been shut…"

Minerva was cut off as the sub shot forward. June screamed as the end of the tube came closer, and she closed her eyes just in case it didn't open and she was going to be smashed to bits.

Somewhere behind her, something sounded like an explosion, but she couldn't be sure if it was coming from behind the sub as it was launched or if it was in one of the rooms she had left.

The sound around the sub changed, and June hesitantly opened one eye. The tube was gone. There was nothing in front of the sub but open water.

She had done it.

She had escaped Trenchland.

CHAPTER FOURTEEN

June had no idea how much time had passed between meeting Maury outside the warehouse and getting into the escape sub, but she figured that, all told, it had to be twelve hours or more. She'd been thinking about the entire time as "that night," but it was probably well into the morning by now, maybe even afternoon. She had no interest in actually determining the time. All that mattered was she was tired, hungry, and thirsty. The thirsty part was ironic, considering that she was still surrounded by water. Maybe there were emergency rations of food and water somewhere in the sub. But before she could so much as unbuckle herself to look around, she fell dead asleep in her chair. Running for your life for hours at a time had a way of draining a person.

Something loud woke her. She looked around, dazed and disoriented, not sure for a moment where she was or how she had gotten there. For a short blissful time her mind had shut down against all the horrors she had witnessed. They came back to her quickly, though, when she realized she was still deep under the ocean and still very much not out of danger yet.

She undid the seatbelt, still groggy and thinking she might see if there really was any food.

Something enormous slammed against the outside of her sub, shaking the entire thing and knocking her out of her chair. She screamed as she hit the floor.

"I'm sorry, I didn't quite hear that," Minerva said. "Could you please repeat it?"

"What was that?" June asked as she pulled herself back up to her seat. "What hit us?"

Minerva's response was especially cheery. "If you look out the window to your right, you will see an example of *Tusoteuthis*, also known as the Crushed Squid. Tusoteuthis lived during the Cretaceous period, and despite its name it is thought to be more closely related to modern octopi."

June bit back the biting response she wanted to throw at the voice and instead craned her head to look out the window in the direction it had indicated. "Crushed Squid" certainly wasn't the name she would have given it. More like "Crushing Squid," considering the tentacle slithering past the window looked large enough to wrap around the escape sub and smoosh the whole thing with barely a passing thought. Whatever enclosure it had previously been in, it must have escaped during the explosions and collapse. For the moment it didn't look like it was especially interested in her sub, but if this thing had escaped then most of the other exhibits probably had too, and there was no telling what other prehistoric or mythological monsters might be lurking out there with it in the dark.

"Are you able to avoid anything else like that on the way up, maybe?" she asked.

"I'm sorry, but our current escape route is on a fixed path to provide maximum economic efficiency. Deviation from this path will only happen in the event of extreme emergency or if manual controls are enabled."

What June really wanted to do was ask what the difference was supposed to be from the current emergency of escaping a collapsing underwater complex and a theoretical "extreme emergency," but she was one hundred percent certain that whatever answer Minerva gave her, it would sound terrible. The Tusoteuthis swam off into the deep, clearing the view in the window for June to see the outside of Trenchland for the first time. Or at least what was still remaining of it. It was likely she would never fully know what it had been supposed to look like, probably some marvel of engineering that looked far better than it functioned. Now, however, it looked like half of a giant flat disc inserted into the side of a rocky sea mount. There were struts that had apparently supported it, but most of them were crumpled and torn as pieces of the complex continued to break off and vanish into the deepest parts of the darkness. Judging from the current amount of damage and the rate at which it was breaking apart, she guessed she couldn't have been asleep for more than a few minutes.

"Is there anything else like that that escaped from the complex?" June asked Minerva.

"I'm sorry. I don't have sufficient data to answer that question."

"Christ. Then what the hell good are you even for?"

"Please allow me to now enumerate my one hundred and fifty-six possible uses and how to access them. Number one…"

"Please just shut up and don't talk again!" June said. The computer's voice thankfully fell silent.

The sub was moving in a direction that would soon have Trenchland fall out of view, especially since they were noticeably rising. But she could see the complex for long enough to know that someone, either her or Maury in whatever calculations he'd made for destroying the place, had made some critical errors.

Because the squid wasn't the only thing that had escaped. There was enough distance now that she couldn't make out any details or size, but a number of things were swimming up out of holes in the complex that had no earthly reason to be in the ocean anymore. Or possibly ever. One or two were recognizable even from a distance as things she had seen within Trenchland. Others moved too fast or were too small for her to get a good look at them. She thought of Charybdis or the tentacled thing in the dark pit, and she sincerely hoped that anything that had been in a tank or enclosure deeper inside the facility would have no way of making their way out of the collapsing twisted metal and they would be buried at the bottom of the sea, forgotten by everyone and never to be seen again.

Just as the top of Trenchland went completely out of her view, she thought she saw something rise up from it with a more metallic glint than anything else. It suddenly occurred to her – far, far, too late at this point – that she didn't know for certain that she was the only person left alive in there other than Logane and his goons. She had only assumed. She tried to assuage any guilt by thinking what the odds could possibly be that Logane would have left anyone else that was completely innocent of his conspiracy, but she knew she could never know for certain.

Maybe that metal glint was another escape sub. Maybe some other innocent had gotten out.

Or maybe, she suddenly realized, it was indeed another sub, but not belonging to someone innocent at all. Hadn't she assumed, after all, that Logane would have his own personal sub somewhere?

There was no way he could have escaped. None. He would have had to get past the wall of rushing water and the mosasaurus. But the archway she'd gone through hadn't been the only way out of that room. There was also the way she had come in, and those tunnels and back hallways could have gone to any number of places she hadn't had the chance to see or explore.

It shouldn't matter. Even if Dom Logane or any of his mercs had escaped, all of this would be over once she was on the surface and told the world everything she'd seen. He was probably dead after...

Something hit her sub again, something that rang with a metallic sound that hadn't been there when the squid had run into her. She looked off to the side of the window.

There was another sub next to hers. It was moving away from her, and then coming closer again. Again the metal thud sounded throughout the sub, and on the control board in front of her several previously dark lights suddenly glowed red. She had no idea what they meant, but it was pretty obvious they didn't mean anything good.

"Minerva, who the hell is that?" June yelled. "What's wrong with the sub?"

Minerva didn't answer.

"Okay, you can stop shutting up now!"

The computer voice still didn't answer.

"Fine, pout all you want, but I think this counts as an extreme emergency, don't you? Give me manual control of the sub!"

While the virtual assistant still remained silent, two lights on the console changed from yellow to green, which June figured was about as close to an answer as she was going to get. There was a control wheel in front of her very similar to what she had seen on airplanes, of which she'd had a little bit of schooling on a long time ago. Hopefully the controls worked in a similar fashion. She grabbed it and pushed the sub into a steep downward dive and to the left as the other one tried to ram her again. Instead, the rival sub shot across in front of her, moving quickly, but not so quickly that she didn't get a view through the window of the person controlling it.

It was Dom Logane. Of course it was. Because there was no way June's luck would have allowed her to get away back to the surface that easily.

Other fast-moving things flashed around in the water beyond them, things that were definitely too organic looking to be other subs. One of them was the huge lizard-looking whale-like creature she had seen earlier, and as it swam past June could have sworn, although later she would doubt this, that it winked at her.

She wasn't sure what she should be more afraid of at this point: Logane and his homicidal sub driving, or the many things that may or may not be in the water with her.

Should I just go straight for the surface as fast as I can? she thought, but she was pretty sure the answer on that was no. Something about the incredible amounts of pressure on the sub right now being dangerous to her if she went up too quickly. She wasn't sure exactly of the why or how of it, just that a full bore escape upward was a bad idea.

Logane's sub turned some distance away and started coming back toward her. It looked like he intended to try ramming her again, and from what little she could see from the outside of his sub, his looked a lot sturdier than hers. Hers would probably crack open and implode long before his would if he kept that up.

Something else thudded against the sub, something smaller than Logane's vehicle and probably not trying to directly attack her, but something large nonetheless.

His sub is probably faster and hardier than mine, she thought. *Maybe that also makes it a bigger, shinier target.* She couldn't be sure of that, since she hadn't exactly been allowed a good look at what she was getting inside when she'd been escaping, but she had to do something, and that was the only possible advantage she might have.

Instead of trying to turn the sub up to safety, she instead turned it back around and down in the direction of Trenchland.

There was very little of it left as what remained of the complex came back into view. The largest part of the giant flat disk had broken apart and vanished into the trench below, although there was still enough left to see into the rock of the trench's side, where the parts of the complex that had been carved into the trench rather than dangling over the abyss could still be seen, flooded and the occasional spark or flash of light from within. June's first thought was that those lights were electricity from still barely-operating generators, but she supposed it could have just as likely been some kind of bio-luminescent escapees from the various tanks. It was definitely not something she wanted to get closer to and check, yet get closer she did. She realized that the sub was shining some kind of exterior light, making it easier for her to see, but that was probably the last thing she wanted right now. She didn't see any controls marked for the lights, but when she asked the computer to turn them off, it did so without a word.

Something grazed her sub from above, a metallic grinding that told her Logane had caught up to her again but, probably because she had turned the lights out, he had misjudged the angle at which he came at her. Logane's sub soared over her head and beyond, going too fast to turn around.

The sub was like a bright lure. A lure for a very, very big fish.

It came up from underneath out of the depths of the trench. It had looked big when she had first seen it through the glass in the first exhibit room, but now, with Logane's escape sub to give it a sense of scale, the megalodon dwarfed almost any living creature she had ever seen, even those others that had been on display. Its mouth made Charybdis look like a tiny guppy. Its length dwarfed the mosasaurus. Its teeth were infinity sharper than anything those sabretooth herring had.

And it came right up under Logane, its maw wide open, and swallowed the sub whole.

The megalodon didn't pause. It just kept going up. And after a moment to catch her breath, June had the sub do the same. It was finally time to go home.

CHAPTER FIFTEEN

While Minerva thankfully didn't talk again for the rest of the trip back, June was able to get the computer to take back control of the sub and have it autopilot the rest of the way to the surface. June slept some more, and even found some protein bars stuffed in an emergency pack near the back of the sub. There was no more sign of anything from Trenchland, and for that she was grateful.

The sub finally breached the surface a few miles out from where she had been when she started the night, or the day, or however long it had been. It was at that point that the computer ceased doing anything for her, apparently deciding that its primary programing of getting her to safety was now complete. She was able to take the controls then and nudge it in the direction of the nearest dockyard. She was also finally able to get a cell signal again, which she used to call 911 and report a series of murders. She said that she needed to meet a cop at the docks to give her information, but she hung up before the operator could get much more information from her, and when the operator tried to call back she refused to answer. She definitely wasn't going to repeat the whole story any more than she had to, and it was going to be hard enough just to convince one cop that she wasn't crazy, let alone trying to do the same with a nameless operator. Besides, her phone battery was nearly dead at this point. She had been using it a lot throughout her adventure.

A police car was pulling up with its lights flashing right as she pulled the sub up to the edge of one of the docks. While she opened a hatch in the top and crawled out onto the wooden planks, the officer sat staring at her in his car. The flashing lights turned off, but he was too stunned by the bizarre sight for the first few seconds for him to remember that he was supposed to be checking on a reported murder.

Finally he got out of his car and helped her to her feet at the edge of the dock. A second car pulled up behind the first one, and she stood back for an equally long moment to try to understand the bizarre scene in front of her.

"Um, ma'am?" the first officer asked. "Are you the one who called us?"

"Yeah," she said.

"And, uh, where is this murder at?"

"Well, there were a whole bunch of them. And they were out there." She pointed out in the direction of the open ocean.

"They happened on the sea?" the second officer finally asked. "Was this on a ship?"

"No, it was under the ocean. In an underwater theme park that a billionaire was using as a cover to create biological weapons that he would sell to terrorists and nations around the world."

The two officers turned to stare at each other with wide eyes.

"Better call an ambulance in," the officer said. June didn't know why until she remembered that she was bruised, water-logged, and may have had blood on her, either from her or others. "And also a psychologist."

June shrugged at that. She'd expected to be called crazy. Even with the evidence she had gathered, it would probably take a while before she could convince someone in charge that everything she was going to say was the actual truth.

As they waited for the ambulance, June shared her story. She told them who she was, who she worked for, and what she had been doing sneaking around seemingly abandoned warehouses last night, or however long ago it had been. The looks of incredulity on their faces grew steadily harsher as she talked about the secret sub, the vast underwater complex, the missing billionaire, the executions, and, of course, the creatures.

"Ma'am, I'm not saying I don't believe you," the first officer said. "It's just that…"

"Nothing about the story is believable," June finished for him.

"Well, yeah. Pretty much."

The second officer was standing slightly behind the first, and she casually looked up and out across the water. June had her back to the sea, but she had a clear view of the second officer's face as her jaw slowly dropped.

"Hey, Jay?" she said quietly to the first officer.

Jay didn't seem to hear her. "We're going to have to take you into the station, and you'll need to repeat everything that you just…"

"Hey! Jay!"

Jay finally looked over his shoulder at the second officer. "What is it?"

The second officer pointed out at the water. "Look."

Officer Jay looked out where she was pointing, and his face took on a matching expression to hers.

"No way. There's absolutely no way," he said.

June looked behind her at the place where the officers were staring. She understood why he wouldn't believe the sight in front of them, since she herself had been faced with the same thing earlier and had had trouble wrapping her head around it. But there was no denying that what they were seeing was real, and every single person looking out onto the ocean this morning from the harbor would be able to see it.

A single pale, enormous dorsal fin was rising up out of the water. It was scarred and bleeding, likely because of its escape from the wreckage as well as any fight it might have had with the other escaping monsters.

"You know what?" June said to the cop, although he was so enraptured with the view in front of him that there was no indication he heard a thing she said. "Maybe it will be a lot easier to convince people about this than I thought."

Somewhere else out deep in the water she thought she could see splashing from several different sources. From this distance, the splashes would have to be enormous for anyone to be able to see them from shore. Somewhere overhead a news helicopter could be heard, likely getting footage as several very unlikely things made it to the surface of the ocean.

The cops made no attempt to stop her as she stood up from her spot and started walking away in the search for a phone charger or computer. Even though she had every intention of getting to the hospital eventually to check on herself, she had a suspicion that it was going to be a very busy news day, and she had some articles to start writing.

The End

Check out other great

Sea Monster Novels!

Robert J. Stava

NEPTUNES RECKONING

At the easternmost end of Long Island lies a seaside town known as Montauk. Ground Zero on the Eastern seaboard for all manner of conspiracy theories involving it's hidden Cold War military base, rumors of time-travel experiments and alien visitors... For renowned Naval historian William Vanek it's the where his grandfather's ship went down on a Top Secret mission during WWII code-named "Neptune's Reckoning". Together with Marine Biologist Daniel Cheung and disgraced French underwater explorer Arnaud Navarre, he's about to discover the truth behind the urban legends: a nightmare from beyond space and time that has been reawakened by global warming and toxic dumping, a nightmare the government tried to keep submerged. Neptune's Reckoning. Terror knows no depth

Bestselling collection

DEAD BAIT

A husband hell-bent on revenge hunts a Wereshark... A Russian mail order bride with a fishy secret... Crabs with a collective consciousness... A vampire who transforms into a Candiru... Zombie piranha...Bait that will have you crawling out of your skin and more. Drawing on horror, humor with a helping of dark fantasy and a touch of deviance, these 19 contemporary stories pay homage to the monsters that lurk in the murky waters of our imaginations. If you thought it was safe to go back in the water... Think Again!

Check out other great

Sea Monster Novels!

Michael Cole

SCAR

Scar is a killing machine. Born from DNA spliced between the extinct Megalodon and modern day Great White, he has a viciousness that transcends time. His evil is reflected in his eyes, his savagery in his two-inch serrated teeth, his ruthlessness in his trail of death. After escaping captivity, the killer shark travels to the island community Cross Point, where prey is in abundance. With an insatiable appetite, heightened senses, and skin impervious to bullets, Scar kills everything that crosses his path. His reign of terror puts him at war with the island sheriff, Nick Piatt. With the body count rising, Nick vows to protect his island community from the vicious threat. With the aid of a marine biologist, a rookie deputy, and a bad-tempered fisherman, Nick leads a crusade against Scar, as well as the ruthless scientist who created him.

Rick Chesler

HOTEL MEGALODON

An underwater luxury hotel on a gorgeous tropical island is set for an extravagant opening weekend with the world watching. The only thing standing in the way of a first-rate experience for the jet-setting VIPs is an unscrupulous businessman and sixty feet of prehistoric shark. As the underwater complex is besieged by a marauding behemoth, newly minted marine biologist Coco Keahi must face off against the ancient predator as it rises from the deep with a vengeance. Meanwhile, a human monster has decided he would be better off if Coco were one of the creature's victims.

Check out other great

Sea Monster Novels!

Michael Cole

CREATURE OF LAKE SHADOW

It was supposed to be a simple bank robbery. Quick. Clean. Efficient. It was none of those. With police searching for them across the state, a band of criminals hide out in a desolate cabin on the frozen shore of Lake Shadow. Isolated, shrouded in thick forest, and haunted by a mysterious history, they thought it was the perfect place to hide. Tensions mount as they hear strange noises outside. Slain animals are found in the snow. Before long, they realize something is watching them. Something hungry, violent, and not of this world. In their attempt to escape, they found the Creature of Lake Shadow.

C.J. Waller

PREDATOR X

When deep level oil fracking uncovers a vast subterranean sea, a crack team of cavers and scientists are sent down to investigate. Upon their arrival, they disappear without a trace. A second team, including sedimentologist Dr Megan Stoker, are ordered to seek out Alpha Team and report back their findings. But Alpha team are nowhere to be found – instead, they are faced with something unexpected in the depths. Something ancient. Something huge. Something dangerous. Predator X

Printed in Great Britain
by Amazon

44111530R00079